A MOTHER'S

BETRAYAL

NICHOLE MARTIN

VM4: A MOTHER'S BETRAYAL

Printed in the United States of America

ISBN-13:978-0692727591
ISBN-10:0692727590

Printed by Createspace 2016

Published by BlaqRayn Publishing Plus 2016

"WHAT'S UP DOC?"

THE DECISION IS NOT AT ALL UP TO US

BECAUSE BABIES ARE A GIFT FROM GOD

HE CHOOSES THE INDIVIDUALS THAT WILL BE PRESENTED

"So how was your visit with Dr. Obanka?" I asked my mother as she took off her coat. Her eyes slowly flooded with tears.

"What's wrong Mommy?" I asked curiously.

"I lost the baby," she solemnly stated.

"WHAT? Were you bleeding or something? What happened?" I asked, moving in closer.

"No. It wasn't anything like that. The baby's heart just stopped beating," she said as she wiped away her tears.

"Jesus!" I mumbled. I could see that it was killing her to talk about it, so I held back with my questions, headed for the kitchen and grabbed a few sheets of paper towels.

A MOTHER'S BETRAYAL

"Here. Wipe your nose!" I handed her two of the sheets as I dabbed my eyes with the third.

"At first, he put the monitor on my stomach to listen to its heartbeat," she began. "He didn't hear anything, so he did a sonogram. We knew something was wrong after we didn't hear a heartbeat and according to the sonogram's measurements, the baby stopped growing last month."

"So what are you tellin' me is," I whisperd, "is that you've been carrying a dead fetus inside of you for a month? Can't you get sick from that?"

"That's what he said," my mother confirmed, "which is why he scheduled me for a D.N.C at 6:00 tomorrow morning."

Damn. I drifted into my own little world. Could something like this happen to me? What could cause a fetus's heart beat to stop just like that? Was it something she did and if so, what if I make the same mistake?

"Mommy did he say this could have been prevented? Did you do something wrong – like lift a heavy mail bag?" I inquired

"He really couldn't say, but he did mention that he saw fibroids."

"Fibroids?" I asked, slightly confused.

"Yeah," she sighed. "He said that it's a common disease in women, especially black women, and if this really IS the case, then the tumors most likely suffocated the fetus."

Damn! Poor thing, I thought as I shook my head sadly.

Later that evening, she made the trip to Brooklyn and spent the night at Grams's; this way, she could rest longer before undergoing the procedure at Brookdale's Hospital located in the Brownsville section of Brooklyn.

"Alright Mommy, here's my job number. If you think that you're gonna be discharged before 5:00 p.m. just call me and I'll leave earlier. Lee, Sara, put your coats on," I told my brother and my daughter as we prepared to head back to Queens.

"Nish, you think your job is gonna be okay with that?" Grams asked.

"With what?" I asked.

"With you leavin' early?"

"Please," I said, rolling my eyes. "My mother's in the hospital. What can they say to me? Nothing!"

"Okay. Alright," Grams surrendered.

"U-u-u-gh!" My mother moaned as she positioned her hands on her lower back.

"Mommy, what's wrong with you?" I quickly turned to her.

"All of a sudden, I got this sharp pain like a contraction," my mother groaned in response.

"NISHI CALL THE DOCTOR!" Grams shouted.

Before I could even dial the number Grams shouted again.

"LORD – THIS GIRL IS SOAKING WET! TELL THE DOCTOR HER WATER JUST BROKE!"

"U-u-u-gh!" I heard my mother moan again.

"Mommy are you in a lot of pain?" I asked fearfully.

"Yeah. Tell him that I'm having contractions," she grumbled.

"Shit. This girl's about to have this baby!" Grams shouted nervously. "Oh Lord hurry up Nishi!"

A MOTHER'S BETRAYAL

"They have me on hold!" I shouted back at her, my voice matching her nervousness.

"Well at least you don't have to wait until tomorrow to deal with this," I heard Grams tell my mother in the background.

"Hi this is Nishelle - Gladys Maron's daughter." I spoke quickly as soon as I heard the on-duty nurse pick up. "Can you please let Dr. Obanka know that my mother's having contractions and that her water has also broken?"

The nurse asked me to hold for just a few more seconds and came back with the instructions on where to bring her.

"The fourth floor? Alright – thanks," I said as I hung up.

"What did she say?" my mother asked.

"To go to Brookdale's maternity ward right now and Dr. Obanka will meet us there."

Nature completed its course and later that evening, my mother delivered my stillborn sibling.

****

A MOTHER'S BETRAYAL

Not long after my mother's miscarriage, things grew awkward. My mother and I didn't talk as much and she always seemed angry, especially the night when Teddy brought me a Junior's Cheesecake. It all unveiled when I offered her a piece.

"Mommy would you like a piece of cheesecake?"

"For what? I'm no longer pregnant. What do I need to gain all that weight for?" she snapped as she exited the living room.

Damn, I thought to myself, *all I did was offer your black ass a piece of cake; it didn't even have to be all of that just now.*

"Nishi you know that you and she aren't going to be on good terms for a while," Teddy admonished.

"I know," I sighed ruefully. "It's been like this ever since she lost the baby, but I understand. Hopefully, she'll get over it soon because after a while, her harshness is gonna get on my nerves and only God knows the amount of shit that I can take from you AND her too."

My left eyebrow raised as I remembered his confession. He dropped his head. It was obvious that the only thing Mr. Kinetic Energy had learned in Science class was the process of reproduction.

****

Somewhere around my sixth month, I became overwhelmed with stress. Work, the commute to work and my asthma were all wearing me down. I was always tired and forever had headaches. Thoughts of aborting the baby often crossed my mind and I finally admitted it to my mother.

"Nishi you only have three months left to go," she sighed. "You can do it."

"But Mommy I can't breathe," I whined. "Can't take any medicine and I'm just tired. Teddy gets on my nerves with his married ass, so what's the sense in me even havin' his baby?"

"Nishi…are you havin' this baby for him or for yourself?" she questioned me.

"Honestly, I don't even want to have it anymore," I admitted sadly. "Too much drama."

"Fuck him!" my mother barked at me. "And the only thing that's really bothering you IS him anyway. He's the only one that's stressing you the fuck out. You're a strong young lady, so just have the baby and stop talking shit. After the baby is born simply take his lying ass to court for child support!" she finished, sucking her teeth.

"Oh please - more drama," I said, taking a deep breath.

"Well, his ass shouldn't be such a dog," she said dismissively. "You gotta do what you gotta do. Fuck how he feels! He wasn't thinking about you when he got married, now was he?"

RING! RING! Saved by the phone!

"Hello," I said, snatching up the receiver.

"YOU BITCH! YOU AND YOU BASTARD CHUR'RIN WILL NEVER GET ME HUSBAND." Sigh….more drama, I thought, shaking my head.

"IS THAT ALL YOU KNOW HOW TO DO IS OPEN YOUR LEGS AND HAVE BABIES FOR A MARRIED MAN?" MooMoo shouted through the phone.

"Who is that? Is that MooMoo?" My mother reached for the receiver.

A MOTHER'S BETRAYAL

"I got this!" I whispered to my mother and signaled her to back away.

"First of all Teddy wasn't married when I met him and neither were you when you had your two children which means that you also have a couple of bastards yourself. And tell me - why must you always involve innocent kids'?" I asked the MooMoo.

"Dee chur'rin that WE have together are our kids," MooMoo answered smugly. "And you, well YOU chur'rin, including your unborn child belong to YOU. My husband will have nothing to do with you or you bastard chur'rin. So just be looking for you money order in dee mail, because you will no longer see him. If I can't be daye to see what you two are doin' with each other, then you won't see him at all."

"Oh girl give me a fuckin' break," I snorted, "'cause if he really loved you...."

"Please! He does love me. Can't you see that by now?" MooMoo screamed. "Get it tru you fuckin' head. We are married gyul. And if you don't believe me I can send you a copy of our marriage certificate."

A MOTHER'S BETRAYAL

"Nishi just hang up on the bitch!" my mother snapped. She heard Meryl shouting at me through the phone and I guess I didn't move quickly enough, because she suddenly snatched the receiver from my hand and hung it up.

"See! What did I tell you? Just take his ass to court after the baby's born."

I was so tired of the drama.

****

Three months later, my 7 lbs. 9 oz. little boy was born. Pale and very hairy. Now I know why I had so much damn heartburn. Although, the baby appeared healthy and normal, he remained in the hospital for nine days due to a stressful labor. For each day that he remained there, I ran back and forth to Brooklyn to be by his side. This was one way that I'd lose some of the 248 unwanted pounds.

The nurses noticed my regular visits and advised me to rest up. They promised to update me on his feeding times and his intake amount. The objective was to keep the soy - based formula down after each feeding. Although, his stomach had been pumped of the obscurities that appeared on his x-ray, he continued to regurgitate the formula. They said only time would tell. When the nurse called one morning to let me know that Efani was well enough to go home -- words that any concerned mother would want to hear -- I bolted out of that apartment. From then on, his stomach took some time to totally heal but when it did, he ate like a pig.

Unexpectedly, and for the second time around, I had to endure that lengthy waiting process alone as my infant son was being operated on. Like Sara, Efani also underwent surgery at a very young age. The ten hour bilateral inguinal hernia repair was a success. Thanks to another great team of physicians, my baby boy was doing just fine.

I never went back to that hell hole of a job, but I did go back to working as a temp out in Long Island two months after Efani was born. Luckily for me, three months into that assignment, the bank hired me permanently to work in their auto leasing department, but just as things were looking up, I was served with papers to appear in Family Court.

To my surprise, MooMoo had convinced Teddy to file a petition to pay me child support through the courts. I couldn't believe that bubble head had the audacity to insinuate that Sara wasn't his daughter while under oath.

His tune quickly changed when the judge told him that there was a five hundred dollar non-refundable fee to administer a paternity test. The case was solid and the judge undisputedly granted me a percentage of Teddy's weekly income, plus the arrears. Teddy was livid. But WHATEVER.

****

"Mommy don't you wanna move from this old tired apartment?" I asked her one afternoon.

"Yeah, but no time soon," she replied.

"Why not?"

"Because I don't have any money for that right now," she said with much 'tude.

"Mommy, we've been here for like two years now," I reminded her. "How much longer do you think it'll take before you can start saving up some money?"

"I don't know," she shrugged. "Two, three years at the most."

"Two, three years?" I scoffed at her. "So you'd rather..." I stopped mid-rant. "I'm gonna pick up a few First Time Home Buyer's books and we'll look through them over the weekend; I guarantee you'll change your mind then."

That weekend after looking through only two books, her mouth began to water.

"They're nice right?" I suggested, feeling her out.

"Yeah and they're not that expensive either," she agreed.

"And look at the size of these backyards," I pointed out, "more than enough space for the kids' to run up and down without having to worry about some mad man speedin' down the street or jumpin' the curb."

"They're nice, but I still have some bills to pay Nish," she explained.

Turns out, she had some of Ethon's old debt, as well as some of her old college grants that were now judgments, to deal with.

"How much do you owe mommy?"

"About five thousand," she answered.

I thought about that for a moment…along with my regular salary, some occasional overtime and now those child support payments, I had accumulated over eight thousand dollars in my savings account.

"Okay, here's the deal: I was gonna put three thousand towards the house, but if I give you the money to pay off some of your bills do you think you could come up with the other two grand?" I asked her.

"Maybe," my mother responded ambiguously.

"No. Not maybe," I snapped back. "You have to because if we can't prove to the banks that our past accounts are paid in full, they'll never consider us for a loan."

"Why can't we do it this way? You give me the full five and I'll pay you back the two later," she proposed.

"No, because I might not see it again and plus, you remember my credit card that you borrowed to buy Jivasti's band equipment with?" I reminded her. "Well, I'm still making payments on it. So uh, your idea won't be happening."

"You just like to put your money in the bank and watch it grow?" Her question shocked me.

"And what's wrong with that?" I frowned.

"Nothing," she sneered.

At this point, I realized she was trying to analyze my ability to maintain such figures in my account.

"MOVING AHEAD"

SUCCESS... A WORD THAT MEANS TO ME, MUCH MOTIVATION

CONCRETE WORK IS A MUST IN ADDITION TO BEING FAITHFUL

ACCOMPLISHMENTS CAN BE ATTAINED AT ANY TIME

YET IN THE END NOTHING'S BETTER THAN THAT LUMINOUS SHINE

SUCCESS... A WORD THAT MEANS TO ME, MUCH MOTIVATION

"Nish, your Grams called and she wants you to call her back."

My mother informed me one late Sunday morning after returning home from doing some overtime.

"Oh Lord. What does she want - somebody to take her to her mother's?" I asked.

A MOTHER'S BETRAYAL

"No - but just call her. I told her that you hadn't gotten home from work yet and that maybe you could help her."

"Help her? What do you mean - help her?" I started to fret.

"You know her and her gambling habit," my mother reminded me.

"What about it?"

"She claims to be in some sort of trouble. A money jam and so I told her that you might be able to help her out."

"I don't know why you told her that."

"But Nishi she sounded like she really needed it because …"

"So what Mommy! You know that we're tryin' to get our stuff together so we can buy this house," I interrupted her.

"I know, but I figured that you may have some money on the side that could help her out."

"How much does she need?" I asked.

"Five hundred dollars," she responded.

"FIVE HUNDRED DOLLARS!" I shouted.

"How much are you putting in?" I then turned to ask the nervy one.

"Nish. You know that I don't have any money!" She explained.

"So how much is Evelyn and Renee contributing?"

"From what she told me, nothing, because she doesn't want them to know."

"YOU GOTS TO BE CRAZY! So I'm supposed to kick out the entire five? I don't think so!" I snapped.

"Look, just call her and see what she has to say before getting all bent out of shape," my mother suggested. Reluctantly I made the call.

"Hey Grams, it's me Nishi. My mother said that you wanted to speak to me."

"Yeah. I got a little problem here. And these people want their money," my grandmother stated.

"Well, exactly how much do you need?"

A MOTHER'S BETRAYAL

"They told me that if I came up with five hundred then they'd accept the rest in payments."

"The rest? Who are these people and how much do you really owe them?" I asked.

"Some people that I took out a loan with and they talkin' like they're gonna do something if I don't pay them," her voice started to tremble.

"Something like what?"

"I don't know, but they're talking crazy." She stated.

This time she had gotten herself into some real shit with those illegal number runners.

"Grams you know this number playin' has got to stop!"

"I know. This is it! After I pay these people off. This - Is - It!" She stated without a doubt.

I gave her the money and also instructed my mother never to offer my services again. I was not a part of the FDIC program.

"You know what? Instead of me paying you back the three thousand dollars, I could just deduct it from each month's rent until we move outta here."

A MOTHER'S BETRAYAL

My mother suggested to me some weeks later.

"First of all, I never said anything about paying me back and no, that's alright. I'll continue to give you my portion of the rent and we'll just stick to the original plan."

I couldn't understand why all of a sudden she wanted to switch up the money situation because to me it was simple. This led me to believe she had a plan B. That evening I conducted a three way call to enlighten some people on my most recent proposal.

"Ree - hold on! I'm gonna connect Shalon in on the call," I clicked over.

"Shalon, are you there?" I asked.

"Yeah, I'm here Nish."

"Hey Yamaha Mama, what's up?" Renee greeted Shalon.

"I'm chillin' Ree, how's the kids'?" Shalon responded.

"They're fine."

"Alright – listen to this y'all. Remember when I said I was gonna give my mother the three thousand dollars as a down payment on a house – right?"

"Yeah," they acknowledged simultaneously.

"Okay, well it turns out that she's five thousand dollars in debt and has two judgments pending

against her."

"So what does she want? More money from you?" Renee asked.

"Hold up! Let me finish!" I quickly responded.

"Now in order for her to satisfy these judgments, she has to pay them off in full." I continued.

"Your mother is gonna fuck you yet!" Renee mumbled.

"So I said to her, '*Mommy, I was gonna give you the three thousand to put down on the house, but if I give you the money to pay off some of your bills, do you think you can come up with the other two grand?*'" I explained to them.

"Seems fair - so what's the problem?" Shalon asked.

Every so often I would hear Renee moan in disbelief.

"There shouldn't be one. Her black ass is not only getting a contribution towards the house, but she is also getting a chance to pay off her bills that should have been taken care of years ago. Without your offer she wouldn't be able to do any of this," Renee angrily expressed.

"Right! Okay, so we're all on the same page, but do you know what she had the nerve to tell me?" I said.

"What?" Shalon and Renee were in sync once again.

"That instead of her paying me back the three thousand dollars, she could just deduct it from each month's rent."

"Girl. Your mother is tryin' to scam your ass!" Renee voiced.

"Nishi, I don't know why all of this comes as a shock to you because just think – look at how she handled the motorcycle situation. That's your moms. That's just how she is, so the question is - how are you gonna deal with THIS situation?" Shalon pointed out.

"For real..look at how she did me with the school run. She's just a fucked up individual with her Whoopi lookin' ass," Renee vented.

A MOTHER'S BETRAYAL

My mother hated it when Renee called her Whoopi. For whatever reason, she saw it as an insult.

"But the thing is, I never said anything to her about her paying me back," I reminded them.

"From day one, when you told me you and your moms was gonna be doin' this house thing together, I knew there would be problems. But you know your mother," Shalon added.

"Yeah, Shalon I do and I also thought to myself that maybe she's changed."

"She's changed alright – from bad to worse!" Renee' stated in a relaxed tone.

"I kinda think that she has a plan B, but I don't know what it is," I said.

"Think? I KNOW she does. And all I have to say is, I don't think you should buy this house with her Nishi." Renee expressed worriedly .

"Nish, I agree with Renee. I think you should think it through some more before you do something that you'll regret for the rest of your life."

A MOTHER'S BETRAYAL

Shalon supported Renee's statement. I knew what they were saying was all so true, but I just couldn't see her screwing me like that. Not my own mother.

"I don't think she'll do anything fucked up again, but I do know that I'm not givin' her anymore of my money," I made a promise to myself.

"Yeah, I heard that one before. Where did some of your Pell and Tap grants go? Damn sure didn't go towards your education," Renee' recollected. She was so fed up with my mother's deceitful ways.

"Oh and another thing, she said that some guy in Harlem offered to buy the van from her and if he does, she'll give me a percentage of the profits," I then added.

"Don't hold your breath, because I can tell you right now, you might as well just count the money you put into her van as a loss," Renee' stated in that same relaxed tone.

Selling or seeing a profit from the deal didn't really matter to me because I had recently purchased a Ford Probe from one of Renee's friends for six hundred dollars. It had a few scratches and an ugly dent in the driver's side door, but so what, I had a ride & was saving a substantial amount of money on gas.

A MOTHER'S BETRAYAL

"NISH – I GOT COMPANY WITH ME!" My mother announced as she cracked the apartment door open one evening.

For three nights in a row, Bud had slept at the apartment. Having no one to go home to, I suppose could be a little on the lonely side.

"What's up Nish?" Bud greeted me.

"Flicko!" He took the baby out of his walker. Flicko was Efani's nickname given by Bud.

"Hey Bud," I responded.

"Hi Normlin!" Sara happily greeted the bubbled - eyed pussy hustler.

"So Nish - wanna do me a favor?" My mother asked while preparing her stew fish.

"It depends," I replied. From the tone of my voice, she sensed my skepticism.

"Relax! Relax! I wouldn't ask you to do something for me if I knew that you couldn't," she smiled.

"What is it?" I asked.

A MOTHER'S BETRAYAL

"Wanna have me and Normlin's baby?" She spewed. I cocked both my head and left brow.

"You mean me ah fee (I have to) fuck Nishi?" Bud ignorantly stated as he walked in on our conversation.

"No-o-o Normlin," my mother laughed. I silently stood in amazement.

"She could be my surrogate mother. There's something called In Vitro Fertilization; with the use of a man's sperm, the doctors can fertilize an egg IN A LAB then places it in a woman's uterus to carry it throughout the entire nine months," she explained to her rude companion.

"What?" He frowned.

It was apparent that bubble eyes only knew how to rib 'it' and 'hop' around because this guy seriously hadn't recognized how advanced medicine had become.

"I said the doctors will fertilize my egg with your sperm and then place it in the uterus of a woman who is capable of carrying the baby to its full term." She repeated its process in Layman's terms.

A MOTHER'S BETRAYAL

"Oh-h-h-h-h! Because me tink say me wood ah' fee fuck she (I thought I had to fuck her)." The brainless one repeated himself.

"No-o-o sweetheart. The doctors' have a way of doin' things to help out people like me."

Two of Bellevue's consumers had somehow slipped out of their strait jackets and were now in my presence. Why was I so unfortunate to know such crazed out individuals?

"Nah, that's one favor I won't be doin'," I replied.

"But why not Nish? You're still young and strong; plus you just had a baby," she queried my opposition.

"And. What does that have to do with anything?"

"It means that you can carry my baby instead of some stranger. Plus, then I won't have to worry about the baby being born with any diseases or anything else. I'll pay for everything – medical bills and all; I'll even buy you a new car," she carried on.

"Nope! Sorry! Won't do it!"

A MOTHER'S BETRAYAL

"I'll give you a few days to think about it 'cause I know you love your mother and you'll help me out. Won't you baby?" She smiled and rubbed my back.

Crazy bitch! You must be mad! Better go find some other fool.

****

"Girl – your aunt is gone!" I started the phone conversation with Renee' that following evening.

"Why – what happened now?" She queried.

"She's asked me to be her surrogate mother?"

"You lie!" Renee' surprisingly responded.

"Nope. No I'm not."

"When did she ask you this?"

"Last night after she got home with Bud and his dumb ass had the nerve to say, 'do me ah ' fee fuck she'?" I explained.

"YOU L–I-I-I-E!" The flabbergasted one sang.

"Man! I don't know what's wrong with her, but I'm not doing it!" I told my cousin.

A MOTHER'S BETRAYAL

"Ha-a-a-a! Oh. My. God! Wait until I tell my mother this one. Your mother is SICK!" Renee` was convinced.

"That she is ... hold on 'cause somebody's on the next line." I clicked over.

"Hello," I answered.

"Is my man there?" The woman asked.

"Excuse me?" I said.

"Is Normlin there?"

"No he isn't - who's callin'?" I asked.

"This is his girlfriend, the nurse; you've seen me before!"

"Excuse me?" I frowned.

"Is this the mail lady that he's dating?" The woman then asked me.

"Nope. Good – bye!" Immediately, I clicked back over to Renee.

"That was Bud's girlfriend callin' here lookin' for him."

"WHAT?" Renee shouted.

"You heard me! Bud's girlfriend, she thought I was my mother."

"Whuh dee' ahss did you mudda get she self into?" Renee spoke in Caribbean patwa.

"I don't know, but whatever it is - I know she's too old for this shit!"

****

It wasn't long before my mother pulled Bud's whole card. Come to find out, he wasn't only plunging my mother's cesspool. Simultaneously, he managed to jump the bones of two other women and of the two, one of them was also pregnant with his child. The nurse made my mother aware of the third woman and told her that if she hadn't experienced that miscarriage then she and the other woman would have given birth around the same time.

Black 5 Spd. '89 Ford Probe GT. Like new. Only 72k mls.
Asking only $3,000.

If interested contact: John @ 631-789-1111.

A flyer in the cafeteria read. *Damn – this is a good deal. I should buy this car. Give the one that I have to my mother, so she could also start saving on gas.* I thought it through for a couple of days then one evening during my lunch hour, I called that number to inquire about the car.

"This is John - how are yuh! So listen, the car's in excellent condition. It's my wife's car and she bought it brand new, but she wants a bigger vehicle because we just had our first child," was how he started the conversation.

"Oh okay," I responded.

"She really doesn't want to get rid of it because the car is extremely fast and my wife, she's a speed demon. But hey, sometimes you gotta let things go … you know what I mean? Do you know how to drive a stick?"

"Yes."

"Great! So listen, where are you now? 'Cause if it's okay with you I can bring the car over so you can take a look at it."

"That's fine … I'm at work right now, let me give you directions."

"You mentioned that you work for the bank right?" John asked me.

"Yeah."

A MOTHER'S BETRAYAL

"Great! Then I know where you are - your manager and I just had lunch yesterday. I'm the V.P. for channel 55 on the opposite side of the building. It shouldn't take me anymore than ten minutes to get there." John stated.

"That's fine because I'm on my lunch break right now and I have about forty minutes left."

"Great! I'll see you in ten."

After seeing the car, I fell in love with it. The interior was immaculate; it still had the new car smell and it drove like a champ. I had to make this little black car mine.

"See, didn't I tell yuh. Fast – right? Once you shift this baby into second gear and the turbo kicks in, you'll pass everything on the expressway!" John boasted.

"I like it!" I smiled, playing it cool.

"It's been garaged since the day we bought it. It's never been in an accident, has brand new tires and I normally have it serviced every six months. See, these are the service dates and the number to the dealer – if you wanna check it out."

A MOTHER'S BETRAYAL

"Nah – it's okay. I believe you." John was not only the V.P. of a prominent television station, but was also a damn good salesman.

By the end of the month, the car was mine. I gave my first Probe to my mother, but not before I paid to get that ugly dent knocked out and the entire car painted.

She was pleased with the body work, but wasn't too thrilled about the candy red paint job. Red was its original color, but because I wanted the paint job to be flawless, I had the auto body paint the entire car and the red that they used was a tad bit brighter than the original red.

****

Shopping for a house was no joke. We looked for months and finally one caught our eye. A two level, mother – daughter property which consisted of four bedrooms, a huge backyard, 1 ½ bathrooms and an unfinished basement. The living room and kitchen area would have to be shared, but that wouldn't be a problem.

"So ladies, you like the one on Moriston huh?" The agent asked us.

"Yes... so far we have our hearts set on that one," my mother replied.

"But I do have to let you know that there's another mother/daughter pair also interested in this same property and I strongly suggest if you're really serious, you should leave a good faith deposit on it."

"Good faith?" I questioned the agent.

"Yes, for at least one hundred dollars. This will show us that you are serious and it will also prevent us from showing the house to others. We'll take it off the market and start the paper work for the loan," the agent explained. My mother and I looked at one another, but the look on my mother's face concerned me.

"You two decide. I'll give you a couple of minutes. Plus, this will allow me to take the call in the other office. For some reason the receptionist can't transfer any calls to me in this room. But think about it and I'll be right back," the agent then left us alone in the conference room.

"Nish, I don't have any money on me."

"Mommy, how are you gonna leave the house without any money?"

A MOTHER'S BETRAYAL

"How was I supposed to know that they were gonna ask us for a security payment?" The unprepared one stated.

"You never know when the unexpected is gonna happen and that's why you should always have a little cash in your pocket for emergencies," I responded.

"Nishi, I have no money I said!" She was my mother - I loved her and all, but her financial situation was extremely repulsive.

"Look, I have forty on me. On the way here, I noticed a Chase Bank across the street. I'll run over there to use the ATM - I'll be right back."

I stood up and pushed in my chair. Her face lit up like a Macy's firework. Several minutes later, I returned with the $100.00.

"Ah-h-h! Now that's what I call team work," the agent smiled as I handed her the twenties.

What freakin' team? Only two players' and I was the only one scoring. She inserted the money into an envelope and labeled it MARON.

On the way home, my mother couldn't stop talking about how she was finally going to get her house.

"I hope everything goes well with the banks," she stated.

"If not, we'll just keep on tryin'," I responded.

"So Mommy, did you hear anything else from the guy that wanted to buy the van?" I changed the topic.

"Oh! He bought it last month," she answered.

"Last month? Are you serious?"

"Uh huh!"

"Why didn't you tell me so I could have given you the extra key?" I queried.

"He said he didn't need it," she professed. while sitting in the front passenger seat of my car - pretending to search through her purse...

****

August of `98 we moved into our Brentwood home out in Suffolk County, Long Island. For days, the house was nothing but a fire hazard. Boxes were stacked as high as the ceiling preventing us from entering or leaving through the front door. Little by little, we unpacked and eventually, the living room was cleared.

A MOTHER'S BETRAYAL

"I see you installed new carpeting in your kids' room. It's nice. Matches nicely with the paint job you did too. But just make sure when you're all done – it looks good, 'cause when you move out I don't wanna have to hire someone to go over your work." Ms. Lint pockets boldly stated.

"Move out? You must be crazy! I didn't just sign my entire life away at the closing to be movin' again."

"I'm just jokin'. It looks good though – maybe you can paint my room for me too," she smiled.

"Whatever!" I walked away.

We'd purchased the "mother and daughter" property for $119k. During the closing, which was about two hours long, all I heard was, sign here -sign here - sign at the (x) - sign here, both of you sign here and here. Literally, we did nothing but sign next to the x all day. Not only did we get a good deal, but the previous homeowners paid for the closing costs and our agent was honest too. She returned the hundred dollar "good faith" payment to my mother at the end of the closing. Didn't quite understand why she gave it to her when I was the one who handed her the money in the first place, and if I hadn't noticed the exchange, I wouldn't have seen that money again.

A MOTHER'S BETRAYAL

I approached my mother and asked her what was in the envelope she said, 'nothing, it's just a gift from the real estate agency'. Her conscious must have been kicking her in the ass, because in seconds, she handed the envelope to me and had the audacity to ask me for fifty dollars from it. She tried to justify her actions by saying that this deal was about a partnership.

"Congratulations! You two are now homeowners," the agent shook our hands.

"The clerk is usually offered something at the end of the closing," the real estate agent then added.

"Something like what?" My mother asked.

"Like some pocket money for preparing and organizing all of the paperwork. There's a lot of work put into that." Why did my mother turn and looked at me.

"Nish, I don't have any cash on me," she whispered. That's old news. Tell me something that I don't know.

"Will $40.00 do?" I removed two twenty dollar bills from the 'good faith' envelope.

"That's perfect! The young lady who's sitting right over there in the corner of the room... go and give it to her!" Our agent pointed her out. I turned and headed for the back of the conference room.

"Thank you! Thank you so much!" The woman thankfully accepted the money.

"You're welcome," I smiled and walked away.

Over the next several months, I continued to work overtime to furnish not only the kids bedroom but mine as well. Although, my credit had survived the intense scrutiny of the mortgage loan process, it wasn't good enough to finance a $1700.00 bedroom set that I fell in love with. Grams agreed to finance it for me and with my tax return that following year I paid it off. Within six months, I successfully furnished the two bedrooms and put a sound system in my car. I was happy. My kids were happy, and that's all that mattered.

"Nishi, can I show Normlin your bedroom set?" My mother asked one night during Normlin's visit.

"Yeah, but don't make it a habit of showing off my room," I responded.

A MOTHER'S BETRAYAL

"Normlin, come sweetie. Come look at Nishi's bedroom set."

He approached the doorway of my palace.

"Yeah mun - it nice. Very nice!" He voiced.

"Thank you!" I said.

"So when are you going to buy me a nice set like that?" I heard my mother ask Bud as they stood in the living room. It seemed as if every time I did or bought something new, she wanted the same thing. This went for everything. From my bedroom set, to my audio system and even down to the tinted windows on my car. Every time I turned around she wanted something like mine. It was crazy and just didn't seem right, but whatever – no big deal.

"Nish," my mother pushed open my room door.

"Damn! Don't you know how to knock?" I chastised her.

"Knock for what? In my own house?" Now what the fuck is that supposed to mean?

"What do you want Mommy?" I questioned her with an attitude.

A MOTHER'S BETRAYAL

"We might get some company," she said while making herself comfortable on my bed.

"Get off my bed with your street clothes on! I don't know where you've been." I commanded.

"Relax. You ball headed fool and for your information my clothes are clean… ah-h-h-h! This feels so comfortable. I can't wait 'til Normlin buys mine," she babbled on.

"Mommy who's comin' here?"

I wanted her to get to the point so that she could vacate the premises. Throughout the entire time that she was in my room, her eyes roamed as if she were shopping for something.

"What are you looking for?" I grew annoyed.

"Nothing. Your room looks kinda nice. I must say you and Pueblo did a good job. You think that maybe he can paint the whole house for me?" She asked.

Pueblo was my Jamaican/Cuban barber I had known for years. He was forever trying to date me even before I had Sara, but I never gave him a chance because I was head over hills with Teddy. We became really good friends and I felt comfortable around him. But there was one problem. He was married.

Pueblo wasn't my first choice though. This guy named Cyrus was, but because he was chivalrous & showed me much interest, my mother threatened to call the police on him. She told me..

"The next time I see his BMW or Jaguar… whatever he drives, pull up in front of my house again, I'll call the cops."

"For what?" I remember asking her.

"Because."

"Because WHAT?" I grew annoyed.

"Because, I don't like his Bajan fat ass."

"First of all he's not fat, he's solid & why don't you like him again? I snapped my head.

"Because he's a cocky ass!"

"But mommy he's done nothing to you. Is it because he brings me flowers and has class?"

"You heard what I said and, another thing, if you two plan to get married, I'm not coming to that wedding,"

The Black Mamba then hissed. So, in order to avoid the drama, I distanced myself from Cyrus. It was for his own good.

Anyway, I made it painfully clear that Pueblo was not there for her.

"Nope. Pueblo aint doin' nothin' so I guess you better put your man to work. And who's coming here?" I asked her again.

"Normlin. He might move in with us," she responded.

"What? Since when? You know what…if you wanted to live with a man, then why didn't you buy the house with him? I thought the deal was just us and the kids?" I argued.

"It was… I mean it is, but think about it Nish. We need a man here with us. Two women - three kids. What protection do we have?"

"We have Shadow. And mommy please, that's no excuse. We've come this far and now all of a sudden we need a man? I do remember you telling me something about not needing a man to live your life."

A MOTHER'S BETRAYAL

"Oh well, people change as they get older," she smirked.

"What a fine time to change your mind," I angrily stated.

"It happens that way sometimes," she then added. Her brain was definitely deteriorating from the crack and marijuana abuse. She considered no one else's feelings and felt the world revolved around her.

"Whatever! Do what you wanna do and can you get out of my room now?" In my eyes the conversation was over.

Without saying another word, she rose from my bed and left the room. CRAZY ASS! I sat up to reach for my stereo remote. Beneath the stereo were several child support checks. Damn, I hope nosy didn't see them. I must have had at least four of them just sitting there.

Usually, I'd deposit them into the kids' or my account as soon as I received them in the mail, but over the past several weeks, I simply tore off the perforated edge & took a peep to make sure that the dollar amount was correct. Whatever! I'll deposit them by the end of the month - no big deal. I resumed my position across the bed and tuned into CD 101.9.

****

Our first winter on the island was a cold one. Each morning our cars and the roads were coated with frost, which made our start very slow and slippery. As the holidays approached, it grew colder.

For Thanksgiving everyone was invited out to Brentwood and it was frustrating because I agreed to pick up the Brooklyn mob. This meant Pueblo, because his license was suspended, plus, Renee and her kids aka Bebe's kids. To my surprise, Renee had two extra heads with her. Paul's (now her ex-boyfriend) teenage mutant Negro nephews was there waiting with her. Each time I saw these kids they had grown bigger. Especially in width.

"HOW ARE ALL YOU BLACK FOLKS GONNA FIT IN HERE?" I shouted as they entered my vehicle.

"Whut's up Pueblo? You chillin' in ah dee front?" Renee spoke the Jamaican lingo.

"Yeah mun. Me nah queez up in ah dee back like oonu," he responded.

A MOTHER'S BETRAYAL

"RENEE! WHERE. ARE. Y'ALL. GONNA FIT?" I voiced loudly.

"Relax nuh mahn, we ah guh manage," she stated and proceeded to get in.

Renee and the four kids squeezed their butts in the back of my two door sports car. Those Pepperpot eatin' individuals had the nerve to complain throughout the entire forty minute ride out to Long Island. The evening went well, but for Christmas it was just going to be me, my mother and the kids.

"Nish, are you buying us a Christmas tree?" My mother asked.

"I thought about getting one today, but why are you so interested - you don't even celebrate Christmas."

"I know, but still we have to make the house look nice and colorful."

"Hypocrite!" I snapped.

"Whatever, just buy the damn tree and make the kids happy!"

"Seems like I'll be making more than the kids happy up in here." I closed the argument.

A MOTHER'S BETRAYAL

That Sunday afternoon, she and I left the house to shop for a tree.

"Where are you going?" I asked as she walked towards my car.

"You're driving your car right?" She asked me.

"No! I'm buying the tree so you can at least drive."

"Come on Nishi. I only have enough gas in my car to get to work this week and plus, your music sounds better than mine."

"You know – you're just a poor excuse for a mother. Without ME there's no YOU!" I told her.

"Oh fuck you! You got that shit twisted," she snapped.

"I don't think so." I assured her. For a while the car was silent.

The conversation definitely had spiraled out of control and those last few words obviously pissed her off.

Whatever!

Our first stop was at a Home Depot.

A MOTHER'S BETRAYAL

"Okay Señora Cheapa, let's go and pick out a tree!" I said as we exited my car.

"Fuck you – you bald headed bitch!" WHOA! Her vocabulary was rather limited.

"What's all that for? You act as if you're not cheap," I responded. Immediately after my response, she shoved me from behind.

"Don't touch me again, 'cause you might find yourself walking home," I warned her.

She had some nerve cursing me out. Was I supposed to just stand there and not say anything?

"Look at this one over here Nish. It's only $59.99," she pointed out.

"Please remind me of the dollar amount that you're contributing," I stated. This time she pinched me.

"No, but seriously – it's big enough for the living room," she continued on as if her actions and words had no distasteful effect.

"It's alright, but look at this one over here. It has more body and it's for the same price," I recognized.

"Okay, so we're getting' this one?" She asked me.

"Correction. I'M getting this one," I responded.

"Whatever wise ass! You might be the only one with a little savings right now, but that's okay 'cause by next year – I'll be back on my feet," she wanted me to recognize.

"That's great! I'm happy for you, now help me pick out the decorations and the lights so we can get out of here." I sensed that my witty responses caused her to grow irritable, she grimaced then rolled her eyes at me.

Up and down the aisles we went picking out various ornaments and lights.

"Nish. Come. Isn't this nice?" She found a black Santa Claus motion figure.

"Yeah it's nice, but not for $29.99 it aint," I said.

"It would be nice if they had a Mrs. Santa to go with it," she continued to search through the boxes.

"Wouldn't it be though?" I responded sarcastically.

"LOOK, THERE'S A MRS. SANTA, oh, but that's a white one. We need a black one."

"WE? You must be buyin' 'em, 'cause I'm not," I told her.

"Come on Nishi - you gonna do your mother like that?"

"Why not? Knowing you - you'll do worse," I mumbled.

"What was that?" She quickly stopped and looked at me.

"Nothing. Just keep walking," I smiled.

As my mother unloaded the shopping cart, I watched the cashier as she rang up the merchandise. First the tree, then the decorations and last but not least - the black Mr. and Mrs. Santa Claus motion figures. Yeah, I still bought them. Whatever! No big deal.

Later that night at about 10:30p.m., I heard her car engine roar. I peeped through my window, but by then she had already entered her car.

"MOMMY WHERE ARE YOU GOIN'?" I yelled from the front door.

"THE BRONX!" She shouted through her closed driver's side window.

"The Bronx, at this time of night?" I asked.

"Yeah. From there I'll go to work. I'll call Lee in the morning."

"Do me a favor and make sure that he gets up on time to feed and walk Shadow," she said and backed out of the driveway. She was on a mission. I could see it in her eyes.

The next evening, after getting in from work, I went upstairs to see my mother.

"So how was your night and how does Bud's house look?" I asked her.

"Empty like hell and I know that he had his other bitch in there too," she claimed.

"How?"

"Because for one, I saw her stethoscope."

"But Mommy, do you really expect him to simmer down just because his wife left him? And if this nurse chic is really paying his mortgage every month like he claims she is, then he's always gonna deal with her," I broke it down.

"Well anyway, someone kept calling his house the entire night, but he didn't answer the phone. It was her – I know it was."

"Who? The nurse?" I asked.

"Yeah. The one time he did pick up, I placed my ear against the phone and heard her say she'd forgotten her stethoscope there."

"So did she come to pick it up?"

"No... he told her he'd drop it off to her first thing in the morning, but anyway Ms. Thing also left her toothbrush in his bathroom."

"How do you know it was hers and not his?"

"Because I made him tell me. But anyway after doing our thing, of course he fell asleep - typical shit. And while he was snoring his ass off, I went to the bathroom to take out my diaphragm and it hit me." She began to smile. What has this fool done now?

"I'm listening," I waited for the punch line.

"I took her toothbrush and wiped it all around my diaphragm," she said proudly.

"That is so foul mommy!" I felt for that woman.

A MOTHER'S BETRAYAL

"Well, she had no business being there."

"Umm! I don't know about you," I grew disgusted.

"Like I said - she shouldn't have been there."

"She'd probably feel the same way about you if she knew that you were in the house. After all she is paying the mortgage right? Anyway - I'm gone."

I said my piece and left Satan sitting on the edge of her platform bed.

****

Some few weeks prior to Mother's Day, my mother sent Bud on his way. Why? She had stumbled upon a vagrant scrotum.

"Renee, you won't believe who my mother came home with tonight," I whispered on the phone.

"Who?" She asked.

"Jivasti." I revealed.

"Jivasti? Bum! Buh! You see dot mahn de'. `Em omeless ta-rah-tid," the wanna be Jamaican stated.

"For real? How do you know?" I asked her.

"Because me see 'em in ah dee tree'in station sleepin' pun the blood cleet ground," Renee added.

"I can't believe her. I wonder if she knows this."

"She has to know. I told Grams and little did I know she knew it already. One of your relatives on Putnam Avenue also saw him sleeping at the Nostrand Avenue subway stop," Renee said in plain English.

"So most likely she DOES know," I said.

What was she up to now? She and Bud had only been broken up for about three weeks and already she has a "bum" in the house.

"She knows... ask her! And if she says that she didn't, she's a liar, 'cause the whole damn world knows," Renee` strongly expressed.

"You damn right I'm gonna ask her. I'll call you tomorrow after I get home from work to let you know what she said."

"Okay, cool. Lickle more sistren," was how Renee ended our conversation.

I felt sorry for Renee'. One week she'd be Guyanese and eating pepper pot and another she'd be a rude gyal from Spanish Town, Jamaica. Make up your mind you sweet potato pie – salmon cake eatin' Yankee.

"Mommy!" I called out to her that next evening. Slowly, she pushed my room door open.

"Can I help you?" She asked with a smile.

"With that smile, I gather that you enjoyed your company tonight."

"Yeah - I did," she was still smiling like an idiot. Could her visit have been that gratifying?

"I heard you givin' him a tour of the house, so did he like it?" I then asked her.

"He said that it was nice," she continued to display her huge choppers.

"So how did he get home?"

"I dropped him off at the LIRR. Look, did you call me in here just to ask me a bunch of damn questions?" She snapped.

"Relax midnight! I wanna know if you know what you're doin'."

"What's that supposed to mean?" Her raised locks rattled. It was okay though, because my cross and garlic were beneath my pillow.

"Do you know that this man is homeless?" I cut to the chase.

"USE TO BE!" She grimaced. So she does know. I calmly shifted my hand beneath the pillow.

"Oh so now it's used to be... Mommy what can this man do for you? He has forty million kids, no job and obviously is looking for a place to live. Compared to where he's been sleepin' this would be paradise to him. Come on now, think about it! It didn't work before, so what makes you think that it'll work now?" I allowed my thoughts to flow.

"People change you know and what's wrong with giving someone another chance. And who says that he isn't working. For your information he does... And he was married. His wife put him out and yet, he managed to get his own place by working as a cook in a restaurant," she defended him.

Yuk! I feel sorry for the people who ate that food.

A MOTHER'S BETRAYAL

"Mommy – all I'm tryin' to say is how do you know he's for real?"

"I'm willin' to try. And if it don't work out, then that's my business." Her eyes appeared somewhat red. For a second, I thought I was gonna have to subdue the devil.

"Alright. If you say so."

Two weeks later, The Blair Witch Project movie was being shown on cable and all three of the kids watched it in my room.

"Lee, wake up!" I shook my little brother.

"Yeah." He said and yawned.

"Come on – go to bed the movie's over."

"Can I sleep in your room until mommy comes back home?"

"For what, you have your own room?"

"But I'm scared," Lee lowered his head.

"Scared of what?"

"The movie. It scared me and plus, mommy's all the way in Brooklyn."

"Brooklyn? For what?"

"She went to pick up daddy. He's movin' in here," Lee explained.

"Movin' in?" I frowned.

"Yeah, she didn't tell you?" Lee asked me. "She came in my room last week and asked me how I would feel if daddy moved in." Funny she could consult with a twelve year old and not with her adult daughter.

"And what did you say?" I then asked my little brother.

"I told her that it didn't matter to me."

"Hmm!" I curiously moaned.

A MOTHER'S BETRAYAL

"IF ONLY I KNEW SOONER (PART 1)"

WITHIN THAT FRIEND THERE'S AN ENEMY

THEY'RE EVERYWHERE, YOUR WORK, YOUR HOME - IT'S A PITY

THEY GRIN IN YOUR FACE AND LAUGH AT YOUR JOKES

BUT AS SOON AS YOU TURN AROUND THEY BECOME DIFFERENT FOLKS

THEIR GOSSIP HAS NO PRICE, THEY HAVE NOTHING BUT LOOSE LIPS

THEY SPEAK HIGHLY OF THEMSELVES, NO ONE ELSE GETS RECOGNITION

THIS PERSON AT SOME POINT BECAME MY ENEMY

BUT WAS SO HEAVILY DISGUISED, THAT THEY COULDN'T BE SEEN

In May of `99, that knotty head so and so moved in. His furniture consisted of one throw rug, some four to five milk crates and one huge D.J. type speaker which they placed in the living room.

"Where's Efani's hoppy horse?" I asked my mother after realizing that it was missing.

"Outside where it belongs," my mother responded.

"What do you mean where it belongs… inside is where it should be, so he can play with it."

"I got tired of lookin' at it and plus, it was taking up too much space." She then added to her senseless comment.

Too much space? What the hell are you talking about – we don't even have a living room set.

"Oh - so this big ass speaker aint?" I grew annoyed.

"Nope. It's not."

"Whatever!" I returned to my domain and tuned into CD 101.9; she wasn't going to drive me crazy.

Usually, this is what I did when I pretty much didn't want to be bothered. I'd tune everybody out and blast the radio. As for my kids, they were straight. As long as Nickelodeon was on, to them, everything was peaches and cream.

A MOTHER'S BETRAYAL

While dusting my dresser, I came across a cassette that I hadn't listened to in a while.

"What the hell!" There was a melted Now and Later candy inside each tape deck.

"SARA AND EFANI COME HERE NOW!" I shouted.

"Who put this candy inside my radio?" The meat-heads stood in silence.

"Who. Put. This. Damn candy in my radio?" I repeated.

"Not me." Sara shook her head no. Efani mimicked her.

"Get out! Get out right now! First it's crayon on my bed head and now candy in my radio. That's it! I'm gonna put a lock on my door and don't even think about asking me to come in here to watch my TV. You have your own room and your own TV so keep your asses outta here." I ran those jokers out.

"NOW I HAVE TO GET THIS GOOEY SHIT OUT. AND IT BETTER NOT BE BROKEN EITHER!" I yelled at them through my closed door.

A MOTHER'S BETRAYAL

That following weekend Pueblo came over and installed my lock.

"Try coming in here now you little fatheads." I dared my children as Pueblo tightened the screws.

"Nishi nah mahn, you must keep the kids' out of your room for real when you are not home, 'cause if you don't the picknee ah' guh mahsh up you furniture," Pueblo warned me.

"Well, it won't happen again 'cause now I have a lock," I responded.

"Pueblo! Can you please come outside to watch me and Efani while we ride our bikes?" Sara politely asked. She loved Pueblo's company over her father's. Sometimes I thought Pueblo came over just for the kids.

"Pabo Come!" Efani tugged on Pueblo's hand.

While the three enjoyed the lovely spring afternoon, I started my Sunday dinner then took a nice long shower. After completely drying off, I cracked the bathroom door and quickly scanned the living room. The coast was clear so I made a mad dash for my bedroom which was only about three feet away, but just as I approached the middle of the hall, he turned and looked dead at me.

A MOTHER'S BETRAYAL

"Shit!" I pouted as I swiftly closed my room door.

Unaware that he was in the living area, I scurried to my room, but something went terribly wrong... the back of the towel came loose. Jivasti had just been mooned. Where the hell did he come from? I didn't hear anyone out there.

While driving Pueblo back to Brooklyn later that evening, I filled him in on my uncomfortable moment. He became annoyed but what could he do. On the way back home, I came to a conclusion as to how I was going to approach my mother to educate her on today's peep show.

"Mommy can you come downstairs for a minute? I wanna talk to you."

"WHAT?" She snapped from the top of the staircase.

Whatever! I'm the one with the problem. I took a seat at the kitchen table.

"First of all, a letter from the mortgage company came last Friday and according to them we're one month late. How's that?" I started out.

"They'll get it. I mailed it yesterday."

"Yesterday? Why yesterday when I gave you my check last week? Come on mommy, don't mess up my credit!" I stated.

"They'll get it I said!" She answered viciously. "Is there anything else?"

"Yes, there is. Is he planning to contribute towards the living expenses now that he's here?" I asked.

"He doesn't have to. He's my man."

"And! That doesn't give him the right to live off of two women with children," I told her.

"He'll contribute," she voiced.

"When?" I asked.

"When I say so."

"Oh NO! This ain't gonna work. If you wanna take care of a grown ass man - then that's your business, but I'm not," I explained to her.

"How are you taking care of him?" She asked me.

"He's livin' here right? And if he's not paying any bills then …there's your answer." I stood my ground.

A MOTHER'S BETRAYAL

"Whether he contributes or not is none of your business," she said.

"Oh no? Well, let me just remind you. I didn't sign a lease before moving in here, I signed the deed and other documents pertaining to a mortgage agreement."

"Sweetheart, you're just a co-signer and if you want a lease - I can get you one," she boldly stated.

"You got a problem!" I laughed at her.

Who is this crazy ass woman standing in front of me 'cause it ain't my mother?

"And since it's like that… you can pay your own phone bill, because I'm tired of dishing out one hundred and some odd dollars every month. And two, I'm cutting back on my portion of the mortgage. Instead of six hundred a month, I'm giving you five and he can pay the water bill which is only forty something dollars every three months; just a little something to break him in. Do you think he has the capability of putting aside thirteen dollars a month?" I broke it down.

"You ain't cutting back on shit!" She threatened.

The mortgage was $1300.00 a month and if I was giving her a check for six hundred a month, responsible for the phone which was always well over $100.00 and paying the water bill, then my monthly expenses on the house alone very well exceeded the $700.00 mark.

"Oh yes I am," I stressed. "And three...I need my privacy! When I come out of my bathroom, I don't wanna be lookin' in your man's face." I saved the best for last.

"What?"

"You heard me. Earlier when Pueblo and the kids were outside, I took a shower and as I exited my bathroom, Jivasti looked me dead in the face."

Her facial expression changed as if I had stabbed her with her own pitchfork.

"Alright. I'll talk to him." She came to her senses.

During that intense conversation, I had gotten a lot off my chest. This was the first time I felt relieved in years.

****

Weeks went by and my mother and I still weren't on good terms. Our communication solely consisted of "hi" and "bye." No. I wasn't the perfect person, but still I didn't spend my day thinking about how I was going to demolish someone's spirit for no apparent reason.

A MOTHER'S BETRAYAL

KNOCK! **KNOCK!** Someone rapped at my bedroom door.

"WHO IS IT?" I shouted.

"It's me. I wanna talk to you for a second."

"The door's open." I invited my mother in.

"What's up?" She smiled.

"Nothing," I replied.

"I knew you were home, I heard the music in your car when you pulled up." For a change she was acting civil.

"So Nish what's up?" She asked me again while displaying her over-sized incisors.

"I know you're crazy and all, but give it a rest sometime." I stated somewhat jokingly.

"Ah-h-h-h, you're so stupid. Listen I need a favor." She stood there staring at me.

Obviously, she was in a playful mood, but at the moment I didn't have a ball for her to chase.

"You listening?" She asked me.

"I'm waiting. What is it?"

A MOTHER'S BETRAYAL

"Jivasti got a job today. I went with him to fill out the application and he starts tomorrow."

"So what's the favor?" I asked her.

"I'll accept the five hundred a month, but can you still pay the water bill? It will help me out until I can catch up with some of my bills and then maybe later, Jivasti can pay it okay?"

I smirked and took a deep breath. "Alright." I agreed to the deal.

"Oh, and here's your mail too. I opened one of your letters by mistake. I thought it was mine."

BULLSHIT!

She handed me three envelopes. One of which was a child support check. There wasn't any mail on the window sill when I came in. Usually, if any mail did come, the first person to get home would remove it from the mailbox outside, take what belonged to him/her and leave the remaining pieces on the living room ledge.

"When I came in I didn't see any mail on the ledge," I pointed out.

"I know...when I came in from work, I just grabbed the entire bundle and took it upstairs with me," she responded. But what was the purpose of her taking it all upstairs?

"How's Pueblo?" She tried to initiate some small chat.

"He's fine," I responded.

"Is he coming over this weekend?"

RING! RING! My phone rang. That installation fee set me back some $200.00.

"Whuh gwan bee bee mudduh?" It was the Jamaican version Renee'.

"Hold on." I told my caller then placed the receiver on my bed.

"Excuse me? Is there anything else that you would like to speak with me about?" I asked my mother.

"No bald head and thanks again." She pulled the door up behind her.

"MY DOOR ISN'T CLOSED, CAN YOU CLOSE THE DOOR PLEASE?" I shouted. CLICK! I heard it connect.

"Renee. I'm back."

"How are you gonna put somebody on hold as soon as you answer your phone?" She complained.

"Shut the hell up! Your aunt was in here," I told her.

"Oh Lord, what did her black ass want? Isn't her room upstairs?"

"She came down here to give me my mail that she so called opened by mistake," I explained.

"Opened? Can't she read?" Renee' voiced.

"That's what I said too and my child support check was in that same stack."

"She probably was holding that shit up to the light trying to see the amount," Renee' speculated.

"Probably! Listen, I just got in not too long ago and I have to feed my kids."

"Oh alright, I'll let you go then. I just wanted to hail you up, because I didn't have time to call you while I was at work. Those nosy bitches at my job be eavesdropping. If anything call me later when you're free," Renee' suggested.

"Okay."

A MOTHER'S BETRAYAL

"Lickle more sistren," she said and hung up.

You'd think that my mother was listening in on my conversation, because just as I hung up, she knocked on my door again.

"I'M COMING OUT!" I yelled. Moments later, we met in the kitchen.

"I meant to thank you for hooking up the sprinkler system too. How much did it cost you?" She asked.

"Don't worry about it - it's part of the house right?"

RING! RING!

"Hold on. I hear my phone ringing again," I jumped up running.

"Now my grass will look as good as my neighbors," I heard her say as I ran towards my bedroom.

"Hello," I answered just before the answering machine did.

"Hey Nishi, what's going on girl?"

"Hey Latoya... nothing much. Just talking to my mother and preparing to feed my kids."

"Oh okay," Latoya responded.

A MOTHER'S BETRAYAL

"Listen, let me call you back," I told her.

"Alright, cool."

Latoya was an ex-coworker and now good friend of mine who was originally from Missouri. Months before we met, she had just moved to New York to be with her high school sweetheart, Blair. They were cool peeps and the black version of Sonny and Cher. She had Blair by at least, 2 inches and when she wore heels, they became Sony and Cher to the 5th power.

"You must be bored," I said as I re-entered the kitchen.

"Why do you say that?" She asked.

"Because you just left my room 5 minutes ago talking and now you wanna talk again.

"Damn, I can't even remember now what I wanted to say to you. Your phone is forever ringing." She commented, as I reheated my leftovers in the microwave.

"You were sayin' something about the sprinkler system." I jogged her memory.

"Oh yeah, but I was done with that part. It was really nothing in particular I wanted to talk to you about; I just wanted to talk," she smiled.

BE-E-E-E-P! The microwave sounded.

"You remember when you asked me if he was real or not?" Was how she resumed the conversation.

"Yeah." I acknowledged her.

"Well, I don't know if he's real and like I said, I'm willing to give him a chance to prove himself. And yes, I was wrong for not telling you that he was moving in. Do you accept my apology?"

"Whatever!" I responded.

"No. Not whatever. Do you accept my apology?"

"Whatever!"

We wouldn't be having this discussion if you would have done it right in the first place ASSHOLE.

"Taking him to apply for a job was the funniest thing," she started a new story.

"And why is that?" I asked her. "SARA AND EFANI COME AND EAT!" I then yelled.

"Because I had to fill out the application for him," she explained.

"What was wrong with his fingers?"

"Nothing. The question is… what's wrong with his reading," she then stated.

"Is he illiterate?" she now had my full attention.

"Well, he's not totally illiterate, but at forty something years old you'd think a person would know how to complete an employment application. That's one of the reasons why he and I didn't make it before. I used to read magazines and newspaper articles to him just so he'd be on top of his current events."

"Did he finish school?" I asked her.

"No. He was the oldest of his siblings and he quit to help his mother raise them or some shit like that," she explained.

"Damn! That's sad," I shook my head.

His cerebrum had functioned just enough to prepare some Mauby which I call the Caribbean Kool-Aid and some Tamarind balls (a sugary spicy, sweet and sour snack) in he mud'duh kitchen.

"So I understand what he's going through and I just want you to be happy for me. Just pray that everything works out between us this time, okay?" She most definitely needed a hug.

"Yeah. Alright." I nonchalantly agreed.

"As soon as he gets his first check, I told him to put it aside so he can start savin' up for a car 'cause this car sharing shit ain't working... Wait! Is that my sweetie I hear pulling up in the driveway now?" She jumped up and ran towards the living room window.

"Yep. It's him. Nish, can I borrow your cable wire, so he and I can watch the movie we rented from Blockbuster?"

"What wire... Oh you mean the one that runs from the TV to the V.C.R?" I asked her.

"Yeah," she shook her head yes.

"How can you rent movies and not have the ability to watch them?"

"I have a cable, but it's not working. I think that stupid ass dog chewed on it." She suspected. I stood up and went for the wire.

A MOTHER'S BETRAYAL

"Hi Nishi," Jivasti greeted me.

He was now sitting at the table as I re-entered the kitchen while holding my audio/video cable in my hand.

"Hey Jivasti," I returned the greeting.

"Here Mommy. You could have this one because I have two and plus, my V.C.R isn't WORKING for some reason and I wonder WHY?" I said strongly while staring at my brats.

"Thanks darlin'," she smiled.

"Gladysth, you stho cheap. I tawt (thought) you said dat you was gonna buy dee wyuh (wire) at dee sto' (store) today." The timid voiced lisper pointed out the obvious.

"Oh Jivasti please! Why spend money when you don't have to."

"But it would be stho much bet'ta if you hahd (had) you own, then you wouldn't have to borrow it from she."

"Don't fret over the little things… are you hungry sweetie?" She rubbed his locks.

Lord only knows what happened to the rest of them. On his head were no more than twelve to fourteen locks.

A MOTHER'S BETRAYAL

He had a receding hairline which made his forehead seem bigger.

"No. I'm okay. I had a late lunch," he responded.

"Okay, so are you…," my mother began to speak.

"But you know what?" He quickly cut my mother off.

"What is it sweetie?" She made me sick with that "sweetie shit."

"Today when I went into dee cafeteria to eat lunch.. Oh gosh! If you see how dee women just sthop and look at me." He was not only ignorant, but he was also vain.

"Well if they ever approach you, you just make sure you tell them you're already taken." She said as they headed for the staircase. *You two are made for each other*! I shook my head.

"Goodnight Nishi," he said before mounting the steps.

"Good night!" I responded then proceeded to wash my dishes.

A MOTHER'S BETRAYAL

Later that week, I called Pueblo at the barbershop to make sure that we were leaving as planned.

"Yes nuh mahn! Me did tell you dat allred'ee. Chuh!" He snapped at me with his hoarse sounding voice.

At first when I met him, I thought something was wrong with his throat; turns out that was how he really spoke.

"What are you gettin' so touchy about? Shit - I just wanna make sure that you made the hotel reservations."

"Nishi. Me say… everyting is taken care of," he assured me.

"Fine! Like I said, I just wanted to make sure..Bye!"

I hung up and right away I called my childhood friend Angelica from Brooklyn, who also now lived in Suffolk County Long Island to let her know that my kids would be staying with her for the weekend as planned.

****

The twelve hour drive up north was long and rainy, and by the time Pueblo, his reckless driving friend and I arrived in Canada for Caribana, the parade was already in progress.

A MOTHER'S BETRAYAL

Although the rain was pouring, those Caribbeans, mostly Indians, drank and danced in the storm as if it were nothing. I couldn't understand why these people partied in such bad weather.

That heavy rain fell for about two hours straight before we decided to leave the Lakeshore Boulevard area. We met up with a female friend of his friend then drove to a nearby hotel and thank God too, my clothes were sopping wet.

"What room are we in Pueblo?" I asked as he stepped away from the clerk at the front desk.

"Dee ooo'man say dem allred'ee book," he responded.

"Booked! What do you mean booked?" I frowned.

"Yeah. She say we juss miss dee last room about fifteen minutes ago."

"I can't believe this shit. But Pueblo, I thought you made reservations?"

The friends looked on as we discussed our situation in the hotel's parking lot.

"Nishi nuh mahn - juss top yuh noise!" The thoughtless one blurted out.

"Noise? What the hell are you talking about - we have no place to stay!" I grew livid.

"Look – me say shut 'tup!" He angrily voiced.

"You shut the fuck up! You bring me way up here to have me wondering about where I'm going to rest my freakin' head?"

The big bellied punk then shoved me.

"Fuckin idiot!" I blurted out. He then grabbed me by my neck and pinned me on the trunk of a parked car.

"Pueblo. Leave her alone!" I heard his male friend say.

"She must shut 'tup when me say so!" Pueblo voiced.

"Fuck off!" I kicked him in the shin. He gripped me firmer and clenched his teeth.

"You ah guh mek me murder you out ere (here)?" He roughly stated.

A MOTHER'S BETRAYAL

At that point, both friends pulled the potbelly beast off me.

"PUSSY!" I shouted as I raised up off that car.

"There's other hotels in this area. We can check them out to see if they have any rooms left," the female friend stated. Everyone looked on as if she hadn't said a word.

"Nishi are you alright?" She then asked me.

"Yeah, but he's a fuckin'...."

"Shoosh… don't say anything else! We already know that men are assholes, but just leave it alone because right now he's feeling really stupid," she whispered to me.

That afternoon we searched high and low for a room, but everything was full or either "too expensive" were his exact words, so we ended up staying in a friend's room of that same female friend. Her best friend was kind enough to share her apartment with us for a WAY cheaper rate. The loser, he literally cleaned the young ladies apartment for the day and a half that we were there. He washed her dishes and vacuumed her floor twice a day as a payoff.

His cheap ass didn't even have the funds to fuel up the car rental nor to buy food for himself during our journey back home. He claimed he only had a Canadian bill left in his pocket.

I was both disgusted and relieved when we returned home. The first thing I did after picking up my kids was call LaToya.

"Do you know that we went all the way up there and didn't even have a place to stay?"

"Are you for real Nishi?" She asked.

"I'm dead serious. He never made the hotel reservation and the fool had the nerve to push me because I got upset and chastised him for his irresponsible act."

"So y'all had a fight too?" She asked surprisingly.

"It wasn't really a fight. The only thing he did was pin me to a parked car, but I swung at him for pushing me."

"So I guess you enjoyed your trip huh?" LaToya teased.

A MOTHER'S BETRAYAL

"Never again! I HAD to give you a quick call to tell you that one. But let me go now because I wanna take a nice long hot shower and relax in my OWN bed. I'll talk to you tomorrow girl."

"Alright - but Nishi, let me just say this before we hang up... I think you should'a kept dating Cyrus,"

She chuckled. *Where is all this chipped wood coming from?* I asked myself as I headed for my bathroom.

The next evening my mother came down to see how my trip went.

"So how was Caribana Nish?"

"It was okay, but it rained the entire time that we were there.

"It rained here all weekend too," she informed me.

"Yeah? Damn! Mommy can I borrow your V.C.R?" I asked her.

"Use the one in your kids room!" She suggested.

"Please! They got crayons and all types of other shit in theirs. Can I borrow yours please?"

A MOTHER'S BETRAYAL

"I don't feel like taking all those wires apart?" She complained.

"Oh please. How hard can it be? You're just lazy. It's only two cables that you have to disconnect."

"Shut! Up! with your thick ass. I'll tell Lee to bring it down." Finally, the negotiation was over.

"Thanks you dried up salt fish." I returned the compliment.

My mother had lost a significant amount of weight after she and Bud had broken up. I tried to fatten her up by baking cookies, cakes and everything else in the book, but for whatever reason, she maintained that extra slim physique. Jivasti also thought she was too slim and tried to fatten her up as well but it wasn't going to happen with that damn sea weed they were buying at the health food market.

****

Weeks passed and I hadn't heard from Pueblo; maybe he was looking into another craft, because that barbering shit obviously wasn't putting enough dinero into his el pocketo.

A MOTHER'S BETRAYAL

"Are you okay baby? Do you want more juice?" I asked Efani one week day morning.

I kept him home from day care because he experienced an Asthma attack on the previous night.

"NISHI!" I heard Jivasti yell. It sounded as if he were in the kitchen.

"YEAH?" I answered.

"COME HERE PLEASE?" I headed for the kitchen. Wait - where is he? I looked around.

"JIVASTI WHAT IS IT?" I asked loudly from the kitchen, still unsure as to where he was calling me from.

"COME!" He yelled from the upstairs hallway.

According to my mother, he was now working the night shift. I slowly climbed the staircase.

"What happened?" I asked him as I ascended the flight of stairs.

"Dis came in dee mail for me today," he projected his voice.

Jivasti was now lying across my mother's bed with one leg bent, in a pair of shorts and with no shirt on.

A MOTHER'S BETRAYAL

"Yuh mud'duh told me dat you alstho had to go to Family Court wit' you churin's fah'duh, stho maybe you could tell me what disth means," he handed me the two paged letter.

"They're just telling you to notify them in the event that you change your address or place of employment and that this is the amount that you have to pay." I explained to him. My mother could have explained this same shit to you butthead.

"Oh, I taught dey was asthkin' me fō mō (for more) money."

"Nah." I shook my head no, handed him back his letter then turned to exit their room.

"TANKS NISHI!" Jivasti loudly voiced.

"Alright." I continued down the hall.

Please negro, put on your britches. This ain't a "bargain gal" shop. Bang mother and daughter for one low price.

Although I didn't want to cause any confusion, I still had to tell my mother about him calling me upstairs to their bedroom while he was half dressed.

A MOTHER'S BETRAYAL

"Alright, I'll talk to him," she stated calmly. "But I'm sure it was innocent, 'cause you ain't even his type."

WHAT!!!! Whatever crazy!

Two days later, Efani was breathing well enough to re-attend day care. He also no longer had a fever.

"Bye baby." I waved at him as he played with his school mates.

"I gave him his medicine already which is supposed to last him for eight hours, but if he starts coughing uncontrollably or throws up, just give me a call and I'll leave work early to pick him up." I told one of his teachers. Honestly, I wanted to stay home with my baby boy a little longer, but I couldn't afford to take more time off.

"Shit! Where are my keys?" I voiced while searching throughout my bag one evening after getting home from work.

"Hi Mommy!" Sara greeted me in the hallway.

Each day Lee's job was to pick Sara up at the bus stop and look after her until my mother got home which was usually about 1 ½ hours later.

A MOTHER'S BETRAYAL

"Where are my keys?" I repeated.

"Mommy you can't get into your room?" Sara asked as she looked on.

"Turn the hallway light on for mommy please," I told my daughter.

"Okay, but Mommy if you don't find your keys, I know how to open your door for you." Sara said to me. I ignored her and continued to search throughout my bag.

"Mommy here's a knife!" Sara had gone to the kitchen and returned with a butter knife.

"Sara what are you doin' with that knife - GO AND PUT IT BACK!" I yelled.

"But this is how Granny gets into your room without your key." My daughter innocently spoke.

"What?" I stopped searching and looked at her.

"I saw her do it before." Sara disclosed. WHAT? That woman is unbelievable!

I'd see splinters on the carpet, but never knew where they came from. And me, like a fool would vacuum the area thinking nothing of it.

A MOTHER'S BETRAYAL

"Look. It's right here in my damn coat pocket." I removed the bundle of house keys and unlocked my bedroom door.

"Sara Come," within moments my baby entered my bedroom. "Close the door please… did you eat the snack that I left in the fridge for you?" I first asked her.

"Yeah, but Lee didn't give me anything to drink," she frowned.

"So how many times have you seen your grandmother open my door with a knife?"

"A lot of times," Sara innocently answered me.

A lot was vague and I wanted to know exactly how many unauthorized entries that this half steppin' burglar had made.

"What? Like three, four times – how many?"

"Two times," my seven year old daughter confirmed.

"Thank you baby… you can go now," I kissed her cheek prior to her running off.

"Mommy can I have some candy?" She quickly turned back.

A MOTHER'S BETRAYAL

"After you and your brother have dinner… let me just change my clothes."

"Okay." Sara happily exited my room.

While switching into a relaxing outfit, I realized my mother's V.C.R was missing from my room. It was situated on the top shelf, directly above my television in the armoire.

"MOMMY!" I yelled upstairs. No one answered.

"MOMMY!" I called her again. Suddenly, at the top of the dark staircase was the silhouette of the bipolar one.

"Whatta you want?" She rudely responded.

"Do you have your V.C.R?" I then asked her.

"Yeah." She responded with a nasty tone.

"But how did you get into my room?"

"I opened your door!" She stated in a nonchalant attitude. Shit! She probably saw those checks.

Once again, I had allowed the support checks to accumulate and was planning to deposit them into my bank account soon, but obviously, I didn't move soon enough. Instead of leaving them flat out on my dresser, this time I placed them beneath the V.C.R just in case she entered my room one day just to "talk."

"No, you didn't open my door, you picked my damn lock and for what?" I snapped.

"Because I wanted my fuckin' V.C.R back!" Slowly she began to descend the staircase. I sensed that she was trying to intimidate me.

"So you couldn't wait until I came home from work?"

"I didn't know what time you'd be in and No..I couldn't." She answered sarcastically.

Bullshit, because every night, I got home at 6:40 p.m.

"Huh!" I laughed her off. "You will never get anywhere with your screwed up ass ways!" I told her.

"Oh yeah? So far I'm doin' okay but your screwed up ways pushed your children's father into marrying another woman," she hissed.

"Well, you know what they say. Things happen for a reason." I shrugged my shoulders.

"Yeah they do, but just not in your favor."

"Whatever!" I about faced and walked away. "Crazy bitch!" I muttered. She was so out of line and living with her was becoming grueling.

"Sara you and Efani hang up your coats while I unpack these groceries." I told my little ones after doing my grocery shopping one Sunday afternoon.

"Okay mommy."

RING! RING! Damn, never a dull moment. I ran to my room.

"Hello," I answered.

"Whut's up? You nah wanna speak to me again?" It was sorry ass Pueblo.

"For what... whatchu want?" I cut all the chit chat.

"Nut'n me just call to say eye (hi) and to see ow (how) the picknee dem doin'."

"We're fine. Are you in the shop now?"

"Nah. Me deh pun dee road." He answered.

"Well, let me call you back because I just came in from Costco's and I wanna put away my groceries."

A MOTHER'S BETRAYAL

"Alright, call me pun me cellular phone."

"Fine." I hung up and re-entered the kitchen, only to find all of my groceries on the floor.

"Mommy why are my groceries on the floor?"

"Because I put them there," she answered as she washed a plate.

"For what? How would you feel if I put the things you eat on the floor?"

"Well, they shouldn't have been there in the first place!" She voiced.

"WHAT?" I contorted my face.

"The table is made for sitting at and eating on. Not for your groceries."

"But mommy, I just put them there. My phone rang immediately as I entered the house & I only went to answer the damn thing." I upsettingly explained.

"Oh well," was how she responded. She didn't give a damn.

"Sara and Efani, I'll finish this up. Y'all go and watch T.V." I instructed my babies.

Quickly, they dropped what they were doing and ran to the back.

"Mommy can me and Efani have some candy?" Sara quickly returned and asked.

"Yeah go ahead... but don't take a lot!" I stated firmly. I need to move that bowl of candy from my dresser before these kids make a meal out of it.

"Mommy what's your problem? First you pick my lock and now you're putting my groceries on the floor," I revisited that week old incident then picked up from where I left off some minutes ago.

"Look, if you don't like the living situation here, then leave!" She stated with a smirk on her face.

"Leave? Like I told you before, I did not sign a lease; I signed a deed..."

RI-I-I-I-ING!

"Hello," she answered her kitchen phone angrily. At that moment, I resumed with the unpacking of my groceries.

"Yeah she's here," I heard her say.

"Here. It's Renee'," she handed me the receiver while rolling her eyes.

A MOTHER'S BETRAYAL

"Tell her I'll call her back on my phone."

"She said she'll call you back on HER phone," my mother relayed the message.

"Alright Bye!" She slammed the phone and proceeded to mount the stairs, but before her ascend, she had one more thing to tell me.

"And make sure you remind Renee' that you have YOUR OWN line." She spewed and batted her eyes.

SHIT! What in the world am I dealing with here? I never knew a snake to blink its eyes...

After unpacking, I went to return everyone's call, but to my surprise the answering machine was blinking. BEEP - I hit the playback button.

"Nish. It's your grandmother. Call me when you get my message." Oh hell no, I'll call you back later.

I then took hold of the receiver and dialed Renee's number.

"Hello," she answered.

"Ree it's me. I had to put my groceries away or else your aunt was gonna put them back on the floor?"

"What the hell is goin' on now? Why is she putting your food on the floor?"

"Because she's crazy." I said. BEEP! "...Someone's calling me, hold on Ree."

"Hello." I clicked over to answer the other line.

"Nishi what's going on? Your mother just called me." Grams seemed somewhat disturbed.

"Well, if she just called you then why are you asking me what's goin' on?" I responded.

"She said that since Jivasti's been there, you've changed."

"I'VE CHANGED? First of all, she put my kids toys out in the damn garage just so his big ass speaker could sit in the living room, my daughter saw her picking my bedroom door lock, she's opening up my mail and now her sick ass is putting my food on the floor... Oh and how can I forget, her man saw me butt naked. Now YOU tell me what's going on?" I stated angrily.

"Well Nishi, I didn't know all of that."

"EXACTLY! You DON'T know what's going on in this house." I huffed.

"Like your mother said, if you hate it there so much then you should just leave." Grams pointed out.

"LEAVE? You sound just like her. How am I gonna leave just like that. My name is on this house and where am I supposed to go after putting so much into this place?"

"Well, your mother said that you are only a co-signer."

"Yeah. A co-signer that's always helping her trifling ass out and for your information do you know what a co-signer's responsibility is?" I asked my grandmother.

"Your mother said...."

"Nope!" I cut her off. "I don't wanna hear what my mother said. It means that I am liable for the payments and property maintenance just as well as she is." I gave her the true definition.

"Look, I don't know what's going on, but since that guy moved in there you two haven't been getting along like you used to. It's just one big mess now," she expressed.

A MOTHER'S BETRAYAL

"Anyway, I have Renee' on my other line, so I'll talk to you later." I told her.

"Oh Renee's on the other line? Tell her to call me." Grams requested.

"Yeah - alright. Bye!" I was so disgusted.

"Okay bye." Grams hung up. Crazy ass! Just like your crazy ass daughter. I pushed the flash button.

"Ree?"

"Da-a-a-m-n! I was about to hang up on your ass," she was obviously tired of holding on.

"Sorry, that was your nosy ass grandmother."

"Oh Lord. What does she want?"

"Gossip as usual. She's tellin' me some shit about my mother said that I've changed since Jivasti's moved in here and how I should leave."

"FUCK JIVASTI! YOU'RE HER DAUGHTER. SEE - THAT'S HER DAMN PROBLEM. ALWAYS PUTTING A MAN BEFORE HER KIDS. WHERE THE FUCK WAS HE WHEN SHE NEEDED MONEY TO PAY OFF HER BILLS AND WHERE WAS HE WHEN HER CAR ENGINE WENT AND YOUR STUPID ASS

GAVE HER FOUR HUNDRED DOLLARS SO SHE COULD FIX THAT SHIT?" Renee' yelled in my ear.

"I totally forgot about that one," I managed to squeeze in a few words.

"I'll tell you where he was... his ass was sleepin' in the fuckin' subway station thinking about where is next meal was gonna come from. Your mother's a fuckin' back stabber. I knew she was gonna do some shit like this to you.... I just knew it!" Renee' was angrier than I was about this whole mix up.

"It's okay though, `cause I wasn't planning on living here for the rest of my life."

"That's beside the point. You're there now and you shouldn't be going through all that bullsh... Hold on Nish, hold on! That's MY next line now." Renee' informed me.

Within two seconds, Renee' was literally back on the phone with me.

"Sssst! That was your grandmother." Renee sucked her teeth.

"What'd she say?" I asked.

"Nothing. I didn't give her a chance to say anything, because as soon as she said, 'hello' I told her that I'd call her back," Renee was a mess.

"You're wrong girl," I laughed.

"How am I wrong? She only called here to see what you and I were talking about and as far as I'm concerned, she's gonna take your mother's word regardless."

"Probably. But who cares because I know what's really going on in here." I sternly responded.

****

Moving on with my life, I met this guy. He wasn't a G.Q. model or anything, but he was nice and my kids liked him. Every weekend we'd either go out with the kids or double-date with friends. This weekend was going to be our fourth month anniversary.

"Nish what are you doin' later?" Toya called me one Saturday afternoon.

"Keith and I are taking the kids to see Toy Story 2 and then we're going to Chucke Cheese's for a while... why what's up?"

"Blair and I were wondering if y'all wanted to go bowling with us tonight, but if you're busy with the kids then we could do it next weekend," she mentioned.

"Tonight's fine. I'll let him know when he gets here."

"Alright, so we'll talk later then - have fun!"

"Okay," I responded and we hung up.

"Mommy somebody's knocking at the door," Sara informed me.

"Okay, I want you to do mommy a favor. Ask who is it... don't open the door just ask who is it?"

"Who is it?" I heard my daughter ask.

"IT'S KEITH MOMMY!" I then looked out my room window while curling my hair and saw his truck.

"OKAY, YOU COULD OPEN THE DOOR NOW!" I yelled to her. As usual, I was running late.

"What's up gorgeous?" Keith entered my room with a huge smile.

"Hey! I'm almost done with my hair. Did you lock the door back?"

"Your mom's did," he responded. Keith was a fish and chip, hot sauce eatin', stone cold American.

"My mother?" I grew puzzled.

"Yeah, your mother opened the door for me. What's that strong smell in the living room?" Keith then asked me.

"Some shit she burns throughout the house every so often," I answered him.

"But why is it so strong though?" He fanned. You could cut that smoke with a knife – it was that thick, foggy and strong.

"Don't know, and believe me I don't like it either. That's why my room door was closed, 'cause the shit is stifling us."

"Hi Keith!" Efani energetically greeted.

"Hey! What's up little man? Are you ready?"

"Yeah. We gonna see Toy Stowee 2 wight?" Efani couldn't quite pronounce the letter R.

"That's right... Tell mommy to hurry up or we'll miss it." Kevin told him.

"No we won't baby." I turned and looked at Efani.

"What's that smell?" Sara entered my room.

"What smell?" I turned to give her one of those 'shut up' looks. I knew what it was, but was hoping that she'd leave it alone.

"I don't know, but it stinks and I'm getting out of here!" She ran out of my room. That kid was going to get me in trouble yet.

It was Keith's breath. He wore braces and had a severe case of Halitosis. One day he had the nerve to ask me why I didn't like kissing.

"'Okay y'all – I'm ready. Sara come on. Get your coat and put it on." I called to her. She had gone into her room and was now watching a show on Cartoon Network.

On the way out, Keith turned and said goodnight to Crispy Satan.

"Enjoy your night Ms. Maron."

"Thank you," she looked on while sitting at the kitchen table. Miserable ass.

A MOTHER'S BETRAYAL

Rumor was, she and Jivasti were scheduled to be married soon...you would think she'd be in her glory and dancing to her own rattle.

After a busy day with the kids, Keith hung at the house until it was time for us to meet up with Toya and Blair that night.

"I hope he's not coming back here!" My mother stopped us on our way out that evening.

"Excuse you!" I voiced. No she didn't just say what I think she did.

"I hope you're going home tonight Keith, because I'm tired of lookin' in your face. I'm sure your mother wouldn't like to see Nishi's face almost every day of the week. What do you think?" Keith & I stood in shock.

"First of all, he's not here every day, and why are you so worried about it - he's not coming to see you!" I said to the Black Mamba.

"I'm not worried, but if I see his face around here again he's gonna get arrested. This is not a hotel."

A MOTHER'S BETRAYAL

Great! Just great! Have him arrested? For what? For installing the flood lights in front of the house that I bought your black ass for Mother's Day? This fool was suffering from a severe case of PAWS (Post - Acute Withdrawal Syndrome) and was the epitome of evil. Wasobi did say, once a crackhead always a crackhead!

"FOR WHAT? AND WHAT ARE THE CHARGES GONNA BE?" I shouted.

"Try me!" She threatened.

"Come on Keith!" We exited the house and entered his truck.

Keith and I went our separate ways not long after that incident and surprisingly, it wasn't because of my mother. Our views on life were totally different. He cussed like a sailor, did not know how to hold his liquor and worst of all, he referred to solid - healthy women such as myself as FAT BITCHES. Yes, he called this solid 5'8, 200lb., twenty – eight year old mother of two, a fat bitch. I'm not going to lie, since we've been living here on laid back Long Island, I did put on a few pounds, but I was far from fat. Funky mouth had to go.

A MOTHER'S BETRAYAL

In February of `00, Pueblo gave me a call. Although he showed his ass something fierce in Canada, he still had a place in my heart. Didn't quite understand why, but maybe it was because he never called me a bitch.

"Hey sweets. What's up?" He started the conversation.

"Nut'n big belly."

"You still ma'ad wid me?" He then asked me.

"Please! That Canada shit is so old already."

"So whut's up wid' yuh Yankee ma'an?" He touched another old topic.

"That's done and over with too."

"After 'em ca'hl you a bitch – yuh dash 'em way?" He laughed.

"Well at least he never placed his hands on me - ass wipe!" I pointed out.

"Lord 'av mercy! Yuh 'nah let dat' one down?"

"Hell no, you big bellied ass punk!" I scorned.

"What me c'yan do for you to forgive me?" He asked.

"You could kiss my black ass."

"Gosh! You some'tin else and NO – me nah kiss yuh black ahss. Me nah do dem foolishness!" He stated.

"Fine! Then you could buy me a new muffler for my car because the noise has gotten louder and another V.C.R for me 'cause this one here doesn't work."

"Bum Buh! All 'a dat?" He began to fret.

"You asked didn't you?"

"But Nishi so much me 'av to do? You know me 'av me sue – sue (an obligated weekly or bi-weekly cash contribution done privately with a group of individuals to save money) to pay and…"

"I don't wanna hear all that shit! This will teach you to keep your hands to yourself." I cut him off.

"Ta - roc - co - clot! 'Dis gyal ah' guh' kill me yet." He mumbled.

KNOCK! KNOCK! KNOCK!

"Hold on Pueblo, someone's knocking at my door."

"What is it?" I opened my door. It was the deranged chameleon.

A MOTHER'S BETRAYAL

"Guess who just passed by the house?" She smiled.

My mother and I hadn't spoken to one another since she put my groceries on the floor and threatened to have Keith arrested.

"I don't know - who?" I responded.

"Bud." She smiled again.

"Oh okay, so what did he say?" I asked the needy one.

"He didn't say anything. He just slowed down, looked and kept on going," she said.

"Aww, he's still in love with you and probably wants his woman back." My sarcastic, and what she viewed as flattering, comment caused all of her heads to rattle.

"PLEASE! I AM a married woman now, so he can get lost." Yep! The spiteful one had captured her very vulnerable prey, sunk her fangs into a hollow male and they eventually 'tied their locks.' A circus wedding is what I called it. Two clowns exchanging vows. I wonder if she ever got a divorce from that Nigerian guy who she married many years ago in exchange for some dough. I heard that

Grams and Lee were the only two family members that attended her charade. Doesn't pay to be a witch!

"I'm on the phone right now, so if anything, we'll talk later." I told her.

"You want something from the store? Jivasti and I are going to Costco," she then asked me.

"Nah, I'm good - thanks."

About a week later, Bud passed by the house again, but this time he stopped. My mother claimed he stared at her and Jivasti and then pulled off.

"What did Jivasti do?" I asked her.

"Nothing."

That figures. Pretty boy didn't want to get any knots on his big ass forehead to go with the matted knots that grew from his scalp. Oh man, all I could do was imagine that look. Would have been a sight for sore eyes.

"So you two just sat in the car until he pulled off?"

"Shit yeah!" She exclaimed.

"Big deal! He's just passing by." I then commented.

"He better find another street to drive down cause I'm tired of him passing by here. If he keeps it up, I'm gonna call the cops on his ass. When he gets arrested he'll be alright."

What's with her and this arresting shit? Must be her new way of damning people.

"Lee, where did you get that ice cream from?" My mother asked her son just as she reached the bottom of the stairs.

"Normlin took me to the store and bought it for me."

He calmly stated while sitting on the window ledge. Lee was forever serious, like Comisario aka Sheriff, his REAL father. Even the ice cream didn't stir him up like it would the typical kid.

"WHAT?" She shouted as Lee continued to lick his cone.

"Lee! Whut tiz wrong wit you? Why are you takin' s'thometin from a stranger when you have a mudda and a fahduh in dee house that you can come to?" Apparently, Jivasti, the jive ass turkey, had overheard the conversation and began to reprimand my little brother. FATHER?

Please... since when? Twelve years later? And fool you ain't his damn daddy.

"Lee, the next time that you see him, keep on movin' okay, because he has a death wish." My mother angrily stated.

Rush hour traffic going eastbound on the L.I.E. that next evening was a bitch during my ride home from work. *Damn! I gotta stop to pick up a jar of spaghetti sauce for the chicken cutlet tonight.*

After picking up Efani from day care, I stopped at our neighborhood supermarket.

"NISHI!" A man shouted as Efani & I walked towards the supermarket's entrance. I looked around, but didn't see anyone. Slowly a black Maxima rolled up next to us.

"HEY FLICKO-O-O! WHUT'S UP? MY GIRL NISHI! WHAT'TUH GWAN?" He spoke loudly as he exited his car.

"Hey Bud." I acknowledged him.

"Your car still looks good." He praised my machine.

He and I once raced like two idiots on the Long Island Expressway and yes, I won.

"Thanks. So does yours!" I returned the compliment, but with a little sarcasm in my voice. Some winters back he crashed his car while racing some guy on the Throgs Neck Bridge.

"Yeah mun – me keep it lookin' crisp," he boasted.

"Normlin, what are you doing around here?" I cut to the chase.

"Me live just up dee road." He looked at me through his three dimensional eye wear. With those glasses one could perform a low budget x-ray.

"Where at?" I questioned him in disbelief.

"For real! Near dee golf course. You remember me nurse friend in 'ah dee Bronx?" He openly asked.

"Yeah, I heard about her."

"She just buy'a 'ouse (house) out 'ere (here) about two munts ago."

His liberated penis apparently was still capable of acquiring an erection cause this man had pussy on credit.

A MOTHER'S BETRAYAL

What kind of woman in her right mind is going to purchase a house and allow this loser to move in?

"Oh yeah? Well, let me be the one to tell you that my mother is threatening to have you arrested if you show your face on our block again, so if I were you, I'd keep away." I informed her ex-lover.

"But Nishi, me luv yuh mudda bah'ad. Bah'ad. Bah'ad. And me would never do anyting to harm she, so me CYAN'T believe that she would do me like that." He spoke pitifully.

"Well, I think she would and she's married now too so..." He took his glasses off then shifted his cap backwards to wipe away the sweat that ran down his face.

"Nishi, yuh seeruss (serious)?" He looked me in the eye. He seemed hurt. I kind of felt sorry for the guy.

"Yeah, so it's time for you to give up." I suggested. He dropped his head for a few moments.

"Nishi you take good care of yourself you 'ear me, and hail Pueblo up for me." Normlin said while re-entering his car.

"Of course, you do the same." I watched on as he slowly exited the parking lot. Poor thing, all he ever wanted in life was an abundance of pussy.

That night I was too tired to brief my mother on me and Bud's unscheduled meet up so I waited 'til that weekend to mention it.

"Mommy, I saw your man earlier this week at the supermarket."

"Who Normlin?" She asked.

"Yeah. He claims that his nurse friend bought a house out here."

"SHE'S A DAMN FOOL! I wonder if he still has his house in the Bronx," my mother grew curious.

"I also told him that you were married now… so I don't think he'll be coming around here anymore."

"You did? And what'd he say?" She asked energetically.

"Nothing really. He wiped his head and told me to take care of myself."

"Ha a-a-a-a! Maybe now he'll leave me the hell alone," she laughed.

"GOTTA GO NOW! I'm going to show these two bush boys how to play badminton." I headed for the backyard.

"JIVASTI WHERE ARE YOUR SHOES?" I yelled across the yard.

Immediately as I stepped outside, I recognized the Rasta man's fully exposed feet.

"COME NUH... I DON'T NEED 'DEM TO PLAY!" He yelled back.

"Alright, but if you step in some dog shit you better keep chasing after that ball." I stated seriously.

"DAHG SHIT? Nah mun. Me nah 'tep in no dahg shit - tell Lee fee come. Em 'ave fee clean dee yard before oonu play." Pueblo stressed.

"I did." Lee appeared from out of nowhere. "I cleaned it up already!"

"A'ooow! Yuh bet'ta! 'Cause me nah...."

A MOTHER'S BETRAYAL

"LOOK PUEBLO - JUST COME ON AND SERVE THE BALL ALREADY!" I got tired of him talking about shit.

"I WILL PLAY DEE WIN'NUH." Jivasti acted as a spectator and kept score.

My mother obviously didn't like the fact that her sweetie was standing on the side, so she stepped out and made an appearance.

"WHY ISN'T MY HUSBAND PLAYIN'?"

"GLADYS'TH GO INSIDE NUH! ONLY AT'LETES ALLOWED OUT HYEY (HERE)." Jivasti joked.

"Is that how you talk to your loving wife?" She walked over to her husband and rubbed his locks.

"JIVASTI ARE YOU KEEPIN' SCORE OR WHAT? I shouted across the yard.

"YEAH! TIZ TREE – ZIP!" Jivasti responded.

"WHO 'AV DEE TREE?" Pueblo asked.

"NISHI." Jivasti answered.

A MOTHER'S BETRAYAL

"COME. SERVE NUH MAHN!" Pueblo seemed to be in a rush to lose.

While Jivasti and my mother chatted to one another, I whipped Pueblo's ass.

"GAME!" Jivasti shouted.

"COME ON JIVASTI. YOUR TURN FOR ME TO BEAT NOW." I laughed.

"NO. I DON'T TINK SO DAHLIN' (darling)," he tied his locks up in one and waited for my serve.

WOP! Over the net, the birdie flew and to the ground it fell.

"WHAT HAPPEN JIVASTI?" I yelled across the yard.

"ME HAVE TO WARM UP FUSS!" He yelled back.

WOP! I served again, but this time he returned the birdie.

"ABOUT TIME!" I shouted out.

For about ten seconds straight, we kept that birdie in the air; we were on a roll.

"YEAH MUN! MY GYAL CYAN PLAY." Pueblo cheered.

A MOTHER'S BETRAYAL

"SHUT UP PUEBLO! JUST BE QUIET BEFORE YOU MAKE ME MESS UP!" I shouted. All of a sudden Jivasti stopped in his place and looked down.

"WHAT HAPPEN?" I yelled over to my opponent.

"I S'THEP IN S'THOME DAHM SHIT OVER HEY (HERE) IN DEE CORNUH. I tawt Lee said 'dat he clean it tup?" Jivasti stated angrily.

"Cheey! Cheey! Cheey! Cheey! Cheey!" Pueblo laughed uncontrollably.

Our game in the backyard was over but we took the fun to the streets. We three athletes lined up side by side to race the full length of the block.

"GLADYS'TH, STAT WE OFF NUH!" Jivasti yelled to my mother.

"ON YOUR MARK - GET SET - GO!" We took off like three black stallions.

"GO MOMMY! GO MOMMY!" Sara shouted.

"WUN MOMMY WUN!" Efani also cheered. I had the best cheering squad ever.

A MOTHER'S BETRAYAL

Jivasti won two of the three races and Pueblo won the third run. As for me, I gained my respect by pushing that knotty head Trinidadian & that potbellied Jamaican to their limits...

****

Things in the house were peaceful, well right up until the day when Jivasti decided to allow a distasteful comment to flow from his lips.

"Nishi's butt is stho big that when she turns dee cornuh of de hallway, you can still see it," he laughed.

I'M SORRY - WHAT WAS THAT?

My mother and I looked at one another strangely. Oh, but it didn't stop there. One weekend afternoon he had some company over for lunch.

"John do you wanna sthee sthome titeezths?"

We heard Jivasti say to one of his geriatric clients while in the kitchen. What is this man's problem? Again, my mother and I strangely looked at one another. Jivasti worked as a counselor with mentally unstable individuals and on this particular day, he was allowed to bring them out for a few hours.

A MOTHER'S BETRAYAL

As I sat at the kitchen table directly across from Jivasti and John. I tried to enjoy my salad but the clown continued on with his act.

"JOHN!" Jivasti shouted his client's name this time. "Do you wanna sthee sthome titeezths?"

"Jivasti, what are you sayin?" My mother confronted her jive ass turkey.

John started to fumble as he grew restless.

"Every time John sthees titeezths, he gets excited." Jivasti laughingly broadcasted. John then bashfully looked up at me. And what did I do? I looked back at him.

"JOHN LOOK AT ME!" Jivasti loudly ordered.

It was evident John wasn't the only mentally unstable individual in the house at that moment. Although Jivasti ordered John to look at him, I was curious as to why he insisted that he and his client make eye contact and so, I looked over at Jivasti too. I wanted to see what this fool was getting at.

As soon as Jivasti had John's undivided attention, Jivasti turned and focused on my chest.

A MOTHER'S BETRAYAL

"Mmm!" I shook my head in disbelief and left the kitchen.

It was a good thing that my mother was there to witness her husband's misconduct, because now I didn't have to explain to her that her man was eye balling my mammary glands. She'd asked me to be happy for her, but what she should have been doing was asking him if he was happy with HER?

That night she knocked on my door to apologize for her husband's rude behavior, right after they hosed themselves down in the backyard. Through my bathroom window I watched Jane and Tarzan as they shampooed their locks and lathered their bodies with a bar of soap. The animal in them finally came out and I'm sure their jungle moment caught our neighbor's attention.

"Nish, I was thinking...maybe we should give a house warming this summer." She suggested after the brief apology.

"When?" I asked.

"In August," she responded.

A MOTHER'S BETRAYAL

"But mommy that's in two months."

"I know. We've been here, what... almost two years now and we never had one."

"Do you have money for that? Because I know you. You'll wait until the last minute and..."

"Look! If I don't, my husband will! She bragged.

"Great! So you're good then. You have it all under control, so why are you comin' to me?"

"Oh come on Nish! You know you gotta invite some of your friends. Pueblo, Toya and her boyfriend. What's his name again? Blake?"

"No, it's Blair," I corrected her.

"Yeah Blair, Toya, Pueblo, Shalon and her boyfriend and whoever else," she continued.

"I should invite Teddy too, so his sorry ass could come and see his kids," I joked.

"Yeah! That would be nice. Invite Rumps too, it will be like old times," she rubbed her hands together.

"Look at you! You're serious," I frowned.

"Yeah, why shouldn't I be?"

A MOTHER'S BETRAYAL

Two months later, we had the house warming. Unfortunately, Pueblo didn't make it. Unknown to me, he hadn't returned from his trip to Jamaica at the scheduled time. However, another foreigner did make it out to our gathering.

"Hi Renee." Teddy greeted her.

"What's up tah'l mah'n? Efani looks just like you - OH MY GOSH!" She was startled by their resemblance.

"Yeah mun." Teddy grinned with his orange teeth. Nothing had changed. After all these years, he was still smoking like a chimney and most likely still gulping down that rum too.

"Hello Nishi." He faced and respectfully greeted me.

"Hello Mr. Ted, how were my directions?" I asked.

"They brought me straight in," he smiled.

"Alright, I'll leave you two love birds alone. Teddy, it's good seeing you." Renee' smiled and walked away.

"Hey Teddy, nice to see that you made it," my mother greeted my children's father.

"Tanks."

A MOTHER'S BETRAYAL

"Look at what I gave you?" My mother then added. "She still looks good right even after having two kids?"

WHAT THE HELL! Oh here we go. The mentally deranged one was starting early.

"There's your son and daughter. Don't you think it'll be wise if you said hello to them?" I changed the topic. *And stop grinning in my face, you Caribbean flavored tall drink of water.*

"Efani." Teddy called to his son. Almost instantly they clicked, but not Sara. She remembered the man for what he was (always missing in action) and maintained her distance.

Everyone that was invited didn't show up, but I'm just glad my friends represented.

"Do you know that your aunt was stashing beers in her bag before they left?" My mother mentioned to me later that next morning.

"How do you know?" I laughed.

"Cause I caught her ass in my refrigerator! And I know Toya's mother got an ear full too."

"Why do you say that - did Evelyn talk to her?" I asked.

"Please! The whole damn night. Her mother will never again talk to another New Yorker after last night's episode. You said her mother's a church goer - right?"

"Uh! huh!" I shook my head yes.

"Yeah. She looks on the conservative side, so when is she going back to Missouri?"

"I think she's leaving sometime this afternoon after church… something like that." I responded.

"So what time did Teddy leave and where did you get those torches from? A lot of people were asking me about them?"

"From Party City," I answered my mother.

"Did they cost much?"

"What do you care? You didn't buy them – did you? And he left about three this morning, but first we took Angelica and her son home then we sat and talked for a bit in front of the house," I explained.

"So what about his kids? Did they enjoy their father's visit?"

"Well, Efani fell asleep in his arms, but you know Sara. She barely said 'hi' and that was it."

"Ha-a-a-a! That's your daughter!" She laughed. "So are you two back together?"

"Goodbye mommy!"

"Wait! Wait! Wait! Did he see your bike?"

"Yes," I responded.

Back in June, I wanted to free myself up again, and so I decided to shop for my second motorcycle. Even with my down payment of $1200.00 I still needed a co-signer and once again, Grams came to my rescue.

"What did he say? Did he like it?"

"Yeah - he said it was nice."

"Yeah – it's nice alright! You have a new vehicle and here I am still driving my same old...."

"Hold on!" I stopped her. "You sound like an idiot. Can my kids fit on that bike with me?" I debated.

"No. But still it's NEW." She obviously had a problem with my 2000 Honda CBRF4.

"Like I said - Goodbye!"

A MOTHER'S BETRAYAL

That weekend went by quickly and that following Monday morning started out just as any other Monday morning. Sluggish.

"Nish, can I borrow ten dollars from you?" She hastily spoke. I looked at her as if she were crazy. There I was hustling to get myself and the kids ready for the day and she chooses to hit me up for some money.

"I only have a twenty," I told her.

"Gimme that and I'll give it back to you by Friday. I have a doctor's appointment after work today and I have a co-payment."

"I don't understand. You have two jobs and yet, you don't have ten dollars?" I questioned her.

"Oh come on before you make me late! I know you have the money. Are you gonna give it to me or what?" She grew impatient.

"Here," I handed her the twenty dollar bill.

"Thanks sweetie!" She ran out the front door. Sssst! She has issues. I continued to get ready.

As the day progressed, I remembered our fun filled weekend - but still I hadn't heard from Pueblo.

A MOTHER'S BETRAYAL

"Why are you lookin' so gloomy?" I asked my mother later that evening.

"The doctors claim it will be impossible for me to have another child." She explained in a melancholy tone.

"Mommy are you still tryin' to get pregnant?" I frowned.

"Well, I figured that since I've gotten my period back, then maybe there's a chance."

"But Mommy - Doctor Obanka already told you that you can't because your uterine tissues are…."

"Yeah. Yeah. Yeah. I know what he said, but there has to be another way," she insisted. This fool was going to kill herself trying to have another baby.

"So far you've had two different doctors tell you the same thing, so how could they both be wrong?"

"Will you do me that favor?" She spoke obliviously.

"You're asking me this shit again? What's wrong with you Mommy? Are you sick?"

"Nothin'. And why do I have to be sick to want another child?" She responded offensively.

"Because. What are you tryin' to do - kill yourself to have this man's baby?"

"No. No - I'm not tryin' to kill myself to have his baby. I want this baby for myself and all I'm asking you is if you would be my surrogate mother?"

"Mommy, if I have any more kids, believe me it's gonna be for myself."

She clenched her glass and vacated the premises. Whatever!

"MOMMY YOUR PHONE'S RINGING!" Sara yelled. Quickly, I ran to my room.

"H-h-hello." I held back a sneeze.

"Hi - Goodnight."

"Hello Mr. Ted," I smiled.

"Why you breedin' (breathing) so?" He asked.

"I was running for the phone and plus, I almost sneezed."

"How was you day?" He asked.

"Fine and yours?"

"It was okay. I just finished up haye and now me about to go home."

"Oh, okay," I stated.

"Where's me kids'?"

"In their room," I answered.

"Let me talk to dem!"

"Hold on!' I held the receiver away from my face.

"SARA - EFANI. COME!" I yelled.

"Who is it?" Sara asked as she entered my bedroom.

"It's your father."

"No. I don't wanna talk to him," she ran out.

"I do! I do!" Efani jumped up and down.

"Here!" I handed him the phone.

"Hi daddy!" He was such a pleasant child and who would have thought that some two years later, he and his father would become so attached.

"Okay. Love you too. Bye!" Efani handed the phone back to me.

"Yeah," I said.

"How's he Asthma doin'?" Teddy asked.

"So far - so good."

"Alright I'll talk to you later, because dee phone is ahxin' fō mō (asking for more) money and me don't have any mō change," he explained.

"Okay."

"So take caye (care)!" He said.

"You too."

CLICK!

Damn that ended fast. I didn't want to hang up. Just hearing his voice on the other end made me fall in love all over again. POW! I smacked myself. I had to snap out of it.

"SCHOOL IS ABOUT TO START AGAIN AND THIS YEAR MY BABY'S GOING TO BE IN THE SECOND GRADE!" I shouted so Sara could hear me.

"School is about to start?" She asked.

"Yep, in two weeks."

"YAY-Y-Y-Y!" She shouted. "I need a new book bag Mommy!" She then added.

"I know. This weekend I'm gonna get all of your supplies and shoes okay."

"Okay," she skipped out of my room.

I played it off good, but really I hated school shopping. The crowds and scattered supplies drove me nuts.

The week seemed to go by slowly. *Thank goodness tomorrow's Friday.* I took off my shoes and sat in my comfortable Ikea chair situated in the corner of my bedroom.

"Here Mommy! Here's the mail," Sara handed me the bulk.

"Thank you baby!"

Mine. Mine. Not mine. Not mine. Mine. I went through the entire stack. The first envelope that I opened was addressed:

Ms. Nishelle A. Maron

41 Moriston Street

Brentwood, N.Y. 11717

A MOTHER'S BETRAYAL

Dear Ms. Maron,

In the past, we have attempted to contact you by phone to set up payment arrangements. Unfortunately, our attempt has failed and we deeply regret to inform you that a past due payment of 4,642.92 is due by November 16, 2000. If not, we will be forced to commence the foreclosure procedure on your property.

Should you disagree and choose to dispute the debt or any portion thereof, you must contact our office within thirty days of this notice. Otherwise, we will consider the debt valid.

Sr. Loan Officer, Mortgage Dept.

WHAT THE HELL IS GOING ON?

I placed the letter back in its original envelope and flopped down in my comfy chair. How is it we owe the bank so much damn money?

"NISHI!" Jivasti called me. *Now what do YOU want*? I hesitated to get up.

"NISHI!" He called me again.

"I'M COMING!" As I turned the corner to head for the kitchen, he met me in the walkway.

"You was on dee phone?" He questioned me.

"Nah. What is it?" I seriously looked him in the eye. I was SO not in the mood.

"You tink you could lend me sthome money until next week?"

WHAT? WHAT THE HELL IS THIS?

"Only twenty - five dollarsth," he requested.

"Do you need it right now? This very moment?" I asked him.

"It would be nice!" He smiled.

"Well, give me ten minutes, 'cause I have to get some change."

"Okay." He smiled again. These jokers acted as if I didn't have any bills of my own. What the hell did I look like to them? Their personalized ATM?

By the time I'd gone to the store and made my way back, my mother had gotten home from work. Jivasti met me at the front door of the house.

"Tanksth darling!" He smiled and stated as I mounted the exterior steps of the doorway.

"Alright," I said and proceeded through the ajar screen door.

A MOTHER'S BETRAYAL

"GLADYSTH. I'LL CALL YOU WHEN I AM ON MY BREAK." He shouted from the door.

"OKAY! BUT WAIT!" She spoke loudly and immediately ran to him.

"Gimme a kiss!" My mother demanded. The Black Mamba smartly moistened his lips with her toxic saliva to keep him disoriented.

"Mommy can I talk to you for a minute?" I asked her as she shut the front door.

"I have your damn money fatty!" She snapped.

"You wish that you were my size Ms. Dry Up AND that's not what I wanna talk to you about here." I handed her the envelope.

"Who opened it - you?" She asked while reading the disturbing note.

"Who do you think? Mommy what's going on?"

"I know Nish and I'm gonna take care of it," she responded.

"When?" I asked her.

"Next month," was her response.

A MOTHER'S BETRAYAL

"Mommy, there's no way in the world you're gonna come up with this money by next month and how is it that we owe them damn near five thousand dollars? You can't possibly tell me those checks didn't reach them by the 15th of each month," I spoke sternly.

"Nishi. I just had to catch up on a couple of my bills, but I promise to make this payment by next month."

"Mommy you're messing up my credit!" I voiced.

"For real Nish! I'll straighten this up," she promised.

"Yeah right! When? On the day they come to put our black asses out?" I raised my left brow.

"Aint nobody gettin' put out. So relax yourself fat ass."

"I am so tired of this name calling shit and you better straighten this out for real!"

"And if I don't?" She placed her hands on her hips.

"Unlike your husband, you'll be homeless for the first time." I raised my left brow again.

"FUCK YOU - FAT ASS!" She stressed. The disrespectful language towards one another had become the norm.

"Whatever Black! You have some SERIOUS issues!" I responded angrily and rolled my eyes.

She then raised her hand to hit me.

"Ahh! Keep your damn hands to yourself!" I told her and walked away. The name calling was definitely getting out of control.

A MOTHER'S BETRAYAL

"IF ONLY I KNEW SOONER (PART 2)"

BECAUSE THEY KNOW YOUR EVERY MOVE

THIS ENEMY IS FIERCE

THIS ENEMY IS HUGE

THEY'VE BEEN AROUND YOU FOR YEARS

*IT HURTS WHEN YOUR ENEMIES ARE PEOPLE
WHO YOU LOVE THE MOST*

*YOU TRUSTED THEM WITH YOUR INNERMOST
SECRETS*

TO THEM YOU FELT SO CLOSE

*IT WAS UNBELIEVABLE WHEN I PULLED BACK
THE CLOTH AND SAW MY*

MOTHER

BOOM! BOOM! BOOM!

I rolled over to the other side of my bed.

BOOM! BOOM! BOOM!

A MOTHER'S BETRAYAL

There it goes again. This time I sat up and looked to see where the noise was coming from. Didn't see anyone or anything, however, I saw that it was 2:30 in the morning.

BOOM! BOOM! BOOM!

I got out of my bed, walked over to my bedroom windows and opened the venetian blinds.

"Hi Nishi!" He smiled.

"Do you have a problem?" I whispered.

"Aww please, just dee dō (door) muhn. Come open dee dō nuh!" He spoke incoherently.

"Whut's up?" The obviously inebriated one greeted me as I quietly opened the front door.

"What the hell do you think is up at 2:30 in the morning? Or should I be sayin', WHO'S up at 2:30 in the morning? Obviously, YOUR drunk ass." I said while yawning.

"Gyul, I missed you so much," he hugged me. Damn – the scent of his cologne woke me up.

"Why is your shirt ripped like this?" I managed to ask him as my face was smothered into his chest.

"Meryl. She stchu'pid fuckin' ahss rip it," he angrily stated.

"So that's why you drove forty – five minutes to see me, because you and MooMoo had a fight? Still a major screw up aren't you!"

"Tut-tee minutes," he responded.

"WHAT?"

"I get haye in tut-tee (thirty) minutes. I did ninety all dee way!" The rum drinker bragged.

"You're lucky the police didn't catch your ass. I shook my head. "You're an idiot you know that?" I then told him.

"Nishi. Please don't do that! Please don't be like she! I just want us to be like befō (before)."

"Now how is that possible Mr. Weddin' band?" I smirked.

"Dat's dee wuss ting that I ever done is marry she. Only if you knew."

"Oh please tell me. We have all morning."

"I wanna lay down," he voiced.

A MOTHER'S BETRAYAL

"Please! That bullshit…" I started to say.

"Please! Me head is hut-tin (hurting) me mun," he claimed. Teddy was known for popping an Excedrin tablet every so often.

"Your head's not the only thing that's gonna hurt if MooMoo finds out that you're out here."

"Fuck she! She needs to get a life!"

"Come on! But if you throw up in my bed, I'm gonna kick your drunk ass."

We quietly entered my bedroom. Instantly, he removed his ripped shirt, loosened his belt buckle then unzipped his pants.

"And make sure that you place your clothes over there on the chair and not on my bed." I instructed him as I climbed back into my bed. When he laid beside me, it was like heaven – but only near a liquor store.

"How much did you drink before you drove out here?" I struck up a conversation.

"I only had two glasses of Back - kuh – dee," he answered. Bacardi. Just as I thought. Bacardi was the only thing that he ever really drank besides the Grenadian Rum.

A MOTHER'S BETRAYAL

"Only two - huh?" I questioned him.

"That's not a lot!" He defended himself.

"NOT A LOT? I can smell it on your breath and it's seeping through your pores... I have a brand new toothbrush. Would you like to introduce yourself to it?"

"Alwight (alright)," he laughed.

When he got out of the bed, those two glow in the dark stilts brought back memories. Gosh, I used to love the hell out of this man.

"How does that smell?" He blew his breath in my face after returning from the bathroom.

"You know it smells better! I just hope that I still have some toothpaste left." I spoke sarcastically.

"S-s-s-s-s-st! He sucked his teeth.

"So tell me... why did she rip your shirt?" I reversed our conversation.

"Nothing really - she's just always on me back about some bullshit. Like tonight, me had a trip. I dropped dee people off at 10:30, and by the time I could park up the bus and clean it out, the time was then about 11:00. The first thing she did when I walk tru dee dōe (through the door) was grab me and ahxin (asking) me, who was me wit, so I push she… told she to get the hell outta me face."

"You pushed her?" I shook my head.

"Yeah mun… Nishi I went straight home after dee trip. She had no reason to act like that," he stated.

"But maybe she thinks you're dealin' with someone else."

"Yeah – YOU!" He pointed out.

"What?" I frowned.

"YOU GYUL! She's always bringing up you name like a damn idiot."

"Oh please!" I rolled my eyes.

"Nishi, since you and me broke up, I've been wuckin' (working) hard because she can't keep a job." Teddy explained.

"What? She has two kids and doesn't work?" I shook my head in disbelief.

"She got some little job now, but every time you turn around she quit' tin'."

"Why?" I asked him.

"I don't know. She wuck tree (three) munts hey (here) - six munts dey (there). She makes me sick!"

"So who pays the bills then?" I then asked him.

"I do. I've been carrying her ass for over a year now and I'm tired of dis shit."

"Well, that's who you chose to be your lawfully wedded wife."

"Shut up!" He rolled over and kissed me.

"Mommy I'm hungry!" Sara said as she stood over me at the side of my bed. I slightly raised my head and squinted my eyes. That Sunday morning sun was shining brightly through my windows.

"I'm hungry too Mommy!" Now both offspring were in my room and standing over me. Teddy pulled the sheets back and exposed his head.

THUMP! THUMP! THUMP! THUMP! THUMP! Sara took off like a bat out of hell.

"Hi Daddy!" Efani jumped onto the bed.

"Morning baby!" Teddy replied and took Efani in his arms.

"Hello," my friend answered her phone.

"Hey missy – what's good?" I started the conversation.

"You're pregnant right?" Angelica immediately responded.

"Girl-l-l!" Was all I could say that mid – November evening.

For several weeks, I kept my delicate condition hush, but could no longer hold it in.

"I knew the moment I saw you two together at the house warming you still cared for one another," Angelica pointed out.

"No. Not really," I said.

"Yeah – bullshit. Tell that to somebody who doesn't know your ass. I don't care how much obeah MooMoo practices; she'll never break that up. It's called love, whether you wanna believe it or not," she clarified.

"Girl, I was not planning on having another baby," I stated solemnly.

"Okay, well did y'all use a condom?" Angelica asked.

"No," I said. "But he pulled out and everything."

"Now Nish. You and I both know that you and Teddy can't use the pull out method. It failed you twice already."

"Ohhh BRO – THERRR, why did I even call you?" I groaned.

"Whatever! 'Cause you know that I'ma keep it real – that's why."

Angelica thought she was the 21st century Socrates. She'd listen carefully, analyze your situation and then convey her thoughts. To her, every statement that left her mouth was the only logical one.

"Girl - three kids? What am I gonna do with three kids?" I voiced.

"Let me put it this way then.. either you keep it or you can give it to your mother, 'cause you know she'll be more than happy to take it."

"Yeah right, but I don't think so buddy," I regained my senses.

"This is November right? So let's see here. November - December - January - February..." Angelica counted. "July! Your baby will be born in the month of July," the philosophical one confirmed.

"Teddy's birthday is in July." I informed her.

"July what?"

"July the 13th." I replied.

"How special! Then he and his newborn can celebrate together. Does he know yet?"

"Yeah, I told him." I answered.

"What did he say?"

"At first, he was shocked and didn't say much, but after I mentioned I didn't want any more kids, he asked me if I were crazy?"

"What did he mean by that?"

"I guess he thought I was thinking to abort. He said having a baby is a blessing and that I'd be crazy to get rid of it."

"But is that what you were thinking Nish?" Angelica calmly asked me.

"No, but right now I'm just thinking about all that damn weight and pain that I have to endure all over again."

"Enjoy it! Enjoy every bit of it, `cause there are so many women out there that want and can't even have a baby for whatever reason. Your mother for one."

"For real! Well, my first visit with the obstetrician is next Monday, so I'll call you and let you know how things go."

"Alright then."

Talking to Ms. Know It All that night was very therapeutic for me. Level headed friends like her are good to have.

From the time Teddy found out that I was carrying another one of his meat heads, he made it his duty to call me every morning before I went to work.

"Hi - Morning!"

"Hey - good morning!" I responded.

A MOTHER'S BETRAYAL

"How's dee baby doin'?" He asked.

"Fine."

"Are you troin' up (throwing up) yet?" I could tell that he was running out of questions on this particular morning.

"No, not yet and please don't curse me," I snapped.

"Alwight - kiss dee kids for me."

"Okay," I responded.

"Take caye (care)," he always said at the end of our conversations and I hated it. Those words just made it seem as if I weren't going to hear from him for a while.

"Nishi, when you get a chance, I want you to sign this for me."

My mother entered my room without announcing herself one Saturday afternoon. She and her Jive ass turkey aka Tarzan had just returned from attending some religious ceremony out in Brooklyn.

"Sign what? And I didn't hear you knock?" I voiced firmly.

"Whatever fatty.... LOOK AT YOUR THIGHS!" She grew amazed.

"Look. What is it that you want me to sign?" I grew annoyed.

"It's just a check the bank sent."

"What is the check for? And why do I have to sign it?" I questioned her.

"Because, both our names are on it and it's just extra money that was sitting in the account, so I guess they decided to send it to us," she replied.

Something wasn't right about this story.

"Well, I'm not signing it and I seriously think you need to send it back to them," I told her.

"Why not?" She frowned.

"Because that money..."

RING! My phone rang.

"Hello," I answered it.

"Whut's up! Whut's up!" It was Pueblo.

A MOTHER'S BETRAYAL

He was back in the states now and was still recovering from a very bad motorcycle accident that almost killed him.

"Listen. Let me call you back in like five minutes,"

I hung up and resumed the conversation with my mother.

"Anyway, as I was sayin', that money's there for a reason. It could go towards the principal or better yet, a payment. Just leave it and let it grow. Send it back!" I told her.

"Look. I ain't ask you all that shit... are you signing it or what?" She grew upset.

"I already told you - No!" I stuck to my guns.

She exited the room with a discontented look on her face. I was not about to put my signature on a check if I didn't know the full truth behind it.

"Hello-o-o-w!" The raspy voiced one answered his cell phone on the first ring.

"No, but call me pun dee shop phone."

"Alright." I pushed the 'end' button, waited for the dial tone and then dialed the shop's number.

A MOTHER'S BETRAYAL

"Hello-o-o-w!" Pueblo answered the shop phone on its first ring.

"What are you doing in the shop? I thought your leg was broken."

"It tiz - but me cyaan't (can't) stay in ah dee `ouse (house) ah'l de'ey (all day)."

"Oh alright - so how's things?" I asked.

"Well - tings are okay," he responded. For several moments we held on without saying anything.

"Me nah ear (hear) no neyes (noise) in ah dee back – where duh pick-nee dem?" He broke the silence.

"In the living room somewhere," I answered.

"Oh… So tell me some'tin Nishi - why did you hin-vite (invite) Teddy fee dee `ouse warmin'?"

"So he could see his kids."

"To see 'em kids? You sure about that?" He said in a rough tone.

"Yeah," I responded.

"So tell me some'tin else. Did you 'ave sex wid 'em again?"

A MOTHER'S BETRAYAL

Oh brother! Aren't you married with children too? All up in my mess. And that is exactly what it was. One big mess. I was looking for love in all the wrong places.

"Look…" I voiced. But before I could even get another word out, Pueblo guessed it.

"KISS ME NECK!" He shouted. "Nishi nuh mahn, but why you gee (give) em a'nuduh (another) piece ah dee puss?"

"It just happened okay," I said.

"OH YEAH?" His hoarse voice rumbled.

"Yeah, that's what I said. And what are you so worried about? Aren't you also married with children?"

"But Nishi, at least me did tell you the troot from dee start."

"Well, since we're so truthful to one another, I think now would be a good time to tell you that I'm pregnant again."

"BUM BUH!" Once again there was silence for several moments. "Nishi - you 'ave no fuckin' ambition, don't call me nuh more."

BLAM!

A MOTHER'S BETRAYAL

He slammed the phone down. BYE-E-E! You'll get over it one of these days dumplin' boy.

Some Friday's later, during my lunch hour, I gave the bank a call to inquire about what really was going on with the house.

"Chase Manhattan Mortgage may I have your full name and loan number please?" The operator asked. I supplied her with that information.

"How may I help you today Ms. Maron?"

"A check was mailed to us a couple of weeks ago and I simply would like to know why, and it's exact amount," I requested.

"Sure. I can help you with that. Let me just review the notes on your account - one moment please." I waited patiently while the representative examined the account.

"Ms. Maron, thank you for waiting. It says here that your escrow check in the amount of $2,427.19 was mailed to you on November 13, 2000, and it cleared on November 23, 2000." The mortgage representative informed me. CLEARED? HOW IN THE HELL?

A MOTHER'S BETRAYAL

"But I never signed that check!" I explained to her.

"You didn't?" We were both now curious.

"No!"

"Well, somebody did. Our records indicate the check cleared," the rep assured me. I was lost for words.

"Ms. Maron, what I'll do is note the account and to help you get a better understanding as to who signed the check, I will have our records department forward you a front and back copy of it okay?" The representative offered me.

"Yes please - thank you."

"And I would also like you to know that this matter can be investigated. The individual who signed this check can be brought up on charges. It's obvious that someone did sign it, and for your protection, from this point on, we can submit a claim to the investigative department on your behalf."

"I'll hold off on that for now, I would just like to see those copies first," I stressed. "I appreciate that information though, but for now I'll hold off on that. I'd just like to see that signed copy first."

"Sure, not a problem. It's my job to inform you of your options. Forging a signature is a federal offense and it's something that we take very seriously here at Chase Bank."

When I received those copies, the signature was almost identical to mine. It was unbelievable! I never told my mother I had a copy of that signed check, and six months later, she approached me with another escrow check. This one I signed for argument sake.

****

As we moved further into the winter, her verbal abuse worsened.

"Every time I see you - your ass is getting fatter!" She viciously voiced one evening.

Now who in their right mind wants to hear crap like that after having a headache throughout the entire day and being around co-workers that weren't taught to cover their mouth when coughing? I had no desire to take part in this undesirable conversation, so I left the kitchen area and waited until the snake returned to its pit.

Dealing with her was extremely vexing. It had gotten to the point where I didn't want to be in the same room with her nor did I want to leave my food in the refrigerator without it being sealed. I didn't trust her - AT ALL. This resulted in frequent fast food buying.

"This is yours Sara and here's yours Efani."

After distributing the seafood Lomein among the kids, I then stacked my plate with crab sticks, French fries and the remaining lomein.

"Can I have some juice Mommy?" Efani asked.

"When you're done eating," I told him. Juice was Efani's best friend.

If I allowed it, his diet would have only consisted of liquids. Juicy Juice and those Capri Sun beverage pouches were his favorites.

"DAMN! Look at all that greasy ass food. Don't you think that you're big enough already." Lee and the reptilian one scoped our plates.

"Granny you shouldn't talk, 'cause you and Lee look like a piece of greasy fried chicken."

"SHUT UP SARA!" My mother shouted. I almost choked on my food from laughing too hard.

A MOTHER'S BETRAYAL

"Yeah, you think that shit is funny huh, when you're not home who does she come to when she wants something to eat or drink? Watch. Next time I'm not giving you shit," she hissed.

"Mommy, what do you expect from the child if she's hearing you disrespect her mother almost on a daily basis?" I schooled her. Although she had many heads, I still did not expect a logical answer from her.

"I'm gonna bust her little ass, that's what I'm gonna do!" My mother angrily stated.

"No you're not!" Sara snapped.

"SARA!" I shouted.

"Yeah, go ahead. Keep it up! I'll come over there and tear your ass up right now!" The scaly one was muscling her way towards my baby.

"Sara, Efani, y'all hurry up and finish eatin' because I'm not tryin' to deal with this crazy ass shit." My food was already cold but the temperature in the kitchen was getting hot.

"If you don't like it here, then get out! 'Cause it ain't enough room here for you and three kids anyway," greasy granny nastily added. Here we go again with this 'get out' crap. Oh, but there's room for HIS pregnant daughter though?

Some few weeks ago, she mentioned to me that one of Jivasti's daughters, who was also pregnant, wanted to move in. That conversation quickly came to a halt right after I asked her if the daughter was okay with bunking with our four legged friend Shadow.

"It's the same shit with you every day. Fat ass this and fat ass that. When are you going to stop?" I asked her.

"Well, it's the truth!" She continued on.

"Mommy Dearest, in case you haven't noticed, I am pregnant again," I voiced proudly. "Something that you will NOT have the pleasure of experiencing EVER again."

"Oh yeah? And your fat ass is carrying that married man's baby again," she tried hard to poison my psyche with her bite.

"Married! Carried! And YOUR last 2 - 3 cases were what? Oh yeah, I remember now - MISCARRIED!" She was a bottomless pit and I couldn't take her shit anymore. I then gathered Sara and Efani's uneaten remains and threw them in the trash can.

A MOTHER'S BETRAYAL

"Come on y'all!" My kids and I went in the back. After this baby's born I'm getting the HELL out of here.

That following morning, Teddy called as usual. Our conversation was less than a minute because I was running extremely late and still had to get my babies ready.

CR-U-U-U-SH!

Just as I opened my bedroom door and stepped out, I crunched down on a small pile of trash that had obviously been placed at my door.

"Who put this shit here?" I angrily stated aloud.

"I did. Next time throw ALL your shit away!" I allowed the cold blooded one to rattle on because throughout the entire night I was having these involuntary chest pains.

That same day, I phoned my obstetrician to fill him in on my very uncomfortable and unexpected occurrences.

"What kind of pain is it? Is it a sharp sudden pain or is it a constant pain?" He asked me.

"Sharp and sudden."

A MOTHER'S BETRAYAL

Within minutes, I was on the phone with the receptionist of a highly recommended cardiologist. She was kind enough to fit me in that doctor's schedule as an emergency patient the very same day.

"It's sharp and sudden," I explained to the cardiologist.

"Where exactly are you having this pain?"

"Right here," I touched the left section of my chest directly below my breast.

He jotted something down in his note pad.

"What you may have is an irregular heartbeat. It's common in women that are expecting, but we won't know for sure until we run a couple of tests."

"Okay," I shook my head acknowledging him.

"How old are you Nishelle?

"Thirty. Almost thirty – one."

"Do you have any other children?"

"Yes. Two."

"And has this ever happened to you before?"

"No. I was fine during my other pregnancies."

"I guess this one's a real kick in the butt then - huh?" The cardiologist joked.

"It seems so," I went along with his dry humor.

"Okay... Follow me!"

On his mahogany desk, he placed his note pad down and at that same time I braced my arm on it to stand up.

"Can you make it?" He reached out to assist me. Probably thought my big ass was gonna snap his expensive furniture in half.

"Yeah. I got it. Thanks," I smiled. I was almost 5 months and already weighing 225 lbs. Not a pretty sight.

"This machine here is called a cardiograph. It records every heartbeat and its changes if there are any," the cardiologist pointed out to me as we entered another room.

"Patty here is our technician and she's gonna set you up for the tests, so I'll see you in a bit?" The doctor lightly tapped me on my shoulder then exited the room.

"Hi Nishelle, this is an easy test. Besides laying still, you don't have to do anything. Right now, I'm just gonna ask you to raise your shirt up a bit so I can attach these patches to your chest and hopefully, we'll get a good reading." *I doubt it Ms. Patty, can't you see all this thick ass skin? Your little suction thingies probably won't work on big momma.*

Unfortunately, I didn't experience any pains while in the office that day, but for two weeks I walked around with their portable electrocardiograph attached to my chest. My instructions were to depress the red button when and if I felt a pain coming on. The device would then automatically transmit the reading to their recording database.

On April 11 2001, Efani's 4th birthday, Teddy came out to Long Island to spend the day with his second family.

"Teddy, don't put a lot of pepper in it," I watched while he made the potato salad. For weeks I was craving this dish and unfortunately, potato salad wasn't a dish that I mastered.

"Y'all ain't finish in this kitchen yet?" Medusa entered the cooking area.

"Teddy come and mix it over here," I said while sitting at the kitchen table.

"You're the chef tonight huh Teddy?" She seemed to be sensible for the moment.

"Yeah - I have to take caye of she for dee time that I'm haye."

"You too? I've been taking care of her since the day she was born and still am." I turned and stared at her something fierce. I can only assume that Teddy knew what was coming next, because he quietly mixed the salad and never looked up.

"How are you taking care of me? If anything - I'm taking care of you!' Was my assertive response.

She stood silently in the middle of the kitchen. "HOW ARE YOU TAKING CARE OF ME?" I asked her again. I wanted to know this one myself. Still no response, but her heads began to rattle and my heart rate increased.

"Idiot!" I rigidly walked out of the kitchen. GRRRRR! She tried to play me in front of my company.

A MOTHER'S BETRAYAL

Later that night, she apologized as Teddy napped in my room. *To hell with you, `cause the damage is already done!*

In the early afternoon hours of April 15th, 2001 – Easter Sunday.

"COME AND GET YOUR KIDS SHIT OUT OF THE LIVING ROOM!" My mother opened the screen door and rudely shouted to me.

"What?" I turned and looked at her.

At the time, I was sitting on the front steps entertaining my neighbor. She and I watched our children ride their bicycles and enjoy the beautiful spring day now that the rain had stopped.

"Come and get this shit out of the living room!" She repeated herself.

"Mommy, give me a few minutes," I said then turned to my neighbor to continue our conversation. Why in the hell did she… and how disrespectful…

"Excuse me Laura!" I stood up and entered the house.

A MOTHER'S BETRAYAL

"MOMMY!" I angrily yelled while pulling the screen door close.

"WHAT?" She shouted from the kitchen.

"What shit are you talking about?" I asked her.

"That shit over there!"

From the kitchen area, she pointed at the kids roller blades and Sara's raincoat that was lying on the floor near the front door. The 4 and 8 year old innocent souls had merely tossed their in-line skates and outer garment to the side in a rush to embrace and celebrate that beautiful day with their friends.

"Seriously mommy? It's Easter! It was raining, it stopped, and they got excited about now being able to ride their bikes."

"And I threw your shit at your door," the irrational one continued on.

"I can't believe that you came out there and did that shit in front of the neighbor," I told her.

"Well, maybe you need to be embarrassed in order to keep the living room clean 'cause I'm tired of this shit!" She exclaimed.

A MOTHER'S BETRAYAL

"What shit? A jacket and a pair of roller blades? Mommy, they're outside playing. What's wrong with you? And have I ever embarrassed you in front of your people and what about that shit over there?" I pointed at Jivasti's unused oversized speaker that had made an impression in the carpet.

"Don't worry about that. It's not like your shit."

"You know what? You got a serious fuckin' problem," I rolled my eyes.

"You're right I got a fuckin' problem and it's YOUR ass. And if you don't like it - GET THE FUCK OUT!" She loudly stated and boldly got up in my face.

"You need to get out of my face mommy!" I told her.

"And If I don't?" She got closer and was now pointing all in my face.

"You - need - to - get - out - of - my – face," I pointed back.

"And - if - I - don't." She poked me in the forehead.

A MOTHER'S BETRAYAL

"Ha! Ha! Ha!" I laughed. "You got major issues," I added and backed away. I wanted to poke her back, but instead I just turned away and headed for my room.

POW-W-W!

The Black Mamba sucker punched me from behind. For thirty one years now, I allowed myself to ignore and tolerate her counterfeit character and loved her like a daughter should, but I couldn't take it anymore. I lost it.

BADOOF!

I struck my mother with my left fist. She stumbled and came back with her right.

SWOOSH!

I ducked. I may be too big to float like a butterfly - but I'm damn sure gonna sting your ass like a queen bee.

BADAOOF!

I hit her ass again and this time with my right.

"No! No! Stop!" Lee entered the house and saw us fighting. Knowing that my strength exceeded his, he ran and grabbed me.

A MOTHER'S BETRAYAL

"Get off of me Lee!" I said and pushed him into the wall. To slay the devil was my intent.

I guess that push into the wall caused my little brother to reconsider his approach because when he got back on his feet, he grabbed his mother this time.

"Why are you holding me? Can't you see that's she's bigger than I am."

POW!

I reached over Lee and caught her ass again. Down they both went. That one was for my unborn child.

"Forget it!" My soon to be fourteen year old little brother surrendered and exited the house.

"YOU BETTER THANK GOD THAT I'M PREGNANT OR ELSE I WOULD HAVE THROWN YOUR FUCKIN' ASS THROUGH THE WALL!" I shouted.

"YOU GETTIN' THE FUCK OUT OF HERE ONE WAY OR THE OTHER. JIVASTI CALL THE FUCKIN' COPS!"

"Gladysth, I don't tink you wanna do dat," his punk ass commented while sitting at the kitchen table.

"I don't care! She's gettin' the fuck outta here - even if I have to lie to those fuckin' cops."

Her blood was tainted. It didn't matter to her that I was her daughter; she simply just wanted to ruin me. Jivasti ignored her and remained seated. The 'jungle book' character sat eating some popcorn from his calabash (the shell of a fruit that can be used as a bowl when totally dried and hardened) throughout the entire boxing match as if it were a flipping exhibition.

"Fuck this shit! You gettin' the fuck outta here," she ran to the kitchen.

"Can you send the cops out here because my daughter's beat'n me up," she told the 911 operator.

"The address is 41 Moriston Street. Black female. Thirty – one. Over 200 pounds - she's a big bitch!" It was obvious that the operator had asked for my description.

Silently, I stood and waited for the police to arrive.

"You didn't want to leave on your own, but you'll be leaving here today," she eagerly stated as she looked through the living room window.

"Shut up bitch!" I angrily told her.

A MOTHER'S BETRAYAL

I entered the kitchen to turn off my boiling eggs that were to be colored by the kids later for the Easter egg hunt, and as I re-entered the living room area, the screen door was aggressively opened.

"Who in here called for police?" One of the two officers loudly asked. From his body language I could tell that he was an 'above the law' type of cop.

"I did!" The very scaly, rapid moving, cunning one stated and began to cry.

"Okay tell me what happened?" That officer seemed to be already in the reptiles wrap.

"This is my daughter and this is my house. And for the past year or so her attitude has made it unbearable to live with and now today she attacks me for no apparent reason."

"YOU'RE A LIAR!" I shouted.

"You!" The cocky officer pointed at me. "Be quiet and let her finish!" He added. His arrogant attitude made me sick.

"For what? She's full of shit!"

A MOTHER'S BETRAYAL

"I'm not gonna tell you again," officer arrogant stated firmly as his partner pulled me to the side.

"I know you're upset and everything, but calm down and tell me your side of the story while he talks to her!" The second officer spoke to me.

I explained to him how the argument started and told him that she threw and landed the first punch as I walked away from her.

"And this isn't the first time that she's beat up on me!" I heard her say from my room.

"SHE'S LYING!" I shouted as I walked back towards the kitchen. "Jivasti tell them that she's lying!" I said to her timid husband. He chose to sit in silence. Efani and Sara were now inside the house, also listening in.

"Nishelle, come back over here!" The second officer told me. "And who's that guy sitting over there?" He then asked me.

"That's her husband. He saw the whole thing from the beginning and he heard her say that she was going to lie."

A MOTHER'S BETRAYAL

"Hey big man - did you hear your wife say that?" The second officer asked Jivasti.

"I don't have anyting to sthay - all I know is dat dey was fight'tin." The nincompoop made me out to be a liar.

"Well, from the damage that I see on this one here, there's no doubt that the other one's getting arrested," officer arrogant concluded.Sara balled up into a fetal position and broke down crying.

"What are you gonna do with her kids?" My mother aggressively asked the officers.

"What do you mean.. what are we gonna do with her kids? They live here too right?"

"Yeah," she responded.

"And you're their grandmother right? So they stay here with you." The first officer said and flipped his pad open to write down some information. The miserable one rolled her eyes. It was evident that she was expecting another outcome.

"Where are you going?" The second officer asked and quickly followed behind me.

"I'm gonna call my kids father so he can come and get his kids," I responded.

"Alright I'll wait right here, but make sure you don't try anything funny like pick up a weapon. Is there a gun in this room?"

"No," I laughed. The officer watched as I dialed the number.

The phone rang out and not even the answering machine took the call.

"Is anybody there?" The officer asked me.

"No, it's just ringing out." I answered him.

"I know it's a bad situation and all, but we have to go now." Lucky for me, the second officer was cool and patient.

"Can I make one more call?" I asked.

"Go ahead - but make it quick!"

I dialed Renee's number hoping that she'd pick up and then could pass the message on to Teddy for me.

"Is anyone answering at that number?" The officer then asked me after several rings.

"Nah," I said.

"Can't say we didn't try," he followed me to the front door.

Damn. Where is everybody? I can't leave my kids with this crazed out bitch. Shit! Who's gonna give Efani his next treatment? What if he has trouble breathing during the night? All sorts of questions ran through my mind.

On April 15, 2001 at 2:15 p.m. I was arrested. Her plan worked. Through the screen door, Efani stood watching as the police drove me away in their squad car.

After the very slow processing phase, they prepared for me to be transported to a women's facility, but not before the uncomfortable trip to the bathroom. Throughout my entire piss, a female officer remained in the reasonably sized bathroom with me.

"I'm not gonna put any cuffs on you and you can sit up front with me," the transferring officer told me.

"Thanks!" I entered his squad car restraint free.

"But make sure you DO put on your seatbelt. Here, let me adjust that for you," he reached over to lengthen the belt. This way it would fit comfortably around me and my unborn.

"Thanks," I displayed a semi-smile.

"No problem."

As we pulled out the precincts parking lot, the officer initiated a conversation.

"Of course I heard about why you were arrested and I think that it's a bunch of crap. According to the arresting officer, your mother called it in, and because her face was lumped up he said it was more of a reason to arrest you, but his partner and I, both think that your mother should have been the one who was arrested. I mean, c'mon, you're pregnant for Christ sake, and too she threw the first punch."

"That's what I told him, but Robocop didn't want to hear the truth."

"Robocop? Haha, that's funny. So how many months pregnant are you Nishelle?"

"Six."

"Wow! And your own mother got you arrested? That's crazy, but listen, when we get there I will have to put the cuffs on you or else I will get in trouble for walking in with a prisoner who's not cuffed."

"I understand," I responded.

"Open your mouth!" The female officer ordered. I opened my mouth.

"Hold out your hands in front of you!" I held my hands out in front of me.

She took off the handcuffs and signaled for me to enter the cell.

BOOM!

She pushed the heavy steel gate close.

"Take off your shoes!" She commanded from the opposite site of the gate.

I took off my shoes and passed them through the six inch square that was situated in the middle of the steel bars. In exchange for my shoes, she slid me a pair of the state's paper slippers.

"Can I get my phone call now?" I knew my rights.

"Sure, as long as it's not logged that you had it already," she went to check. Within minutes, she was back.

"Now you can't call your mother's house, because if it sounds like you're talking to her. I will terminate the call," she said upon returning with the traditional police station desk phone.

"Believe me - I'm not tryin' to call her." When she realized that we were on the same page, she pushed the receiver through the small opening.

"So who are we calling?" She asked while holding the base of the phone in her hand.

"My grandmother."

"What's the number?" I called out the number and watched as she dialed it.

"You have a minute!" She stretched the wire and took a seat in a nearby chair outside my cell.

"Hello, Grams. It's me. I'm sure you've already heard what happened."

"Um hmm!" She hummed.

"Anyway… Do me a favor, call Renee` and tell her to call my job tomorrow to let them know that I'm not coming in and tell Lee to give Efani his Nebulizer treatment. He's supposed to have it every four hours… Lee knows how it works."

"I hope you learned your lesson!" Grams was definitely having one of her doltish moments.

"Excuse me!" I heard her, but I didn't hear her.

"I hope - you learned - your lesson!"

"Anyway. Just relay those messages for me," I pushed the receiver back through the hole. My minute wasn't even up yet, but I wasn't trying to hear her crazy ass shit, because her daughter was crazy enough for me.

I sat down and looked around. I couldn't believe it. I was in jail. I had never been arrested and just some years ago, I was hoping of becoming an enforcer of the law. In my cell was a 5 foot long wooden bench no wider than two feet that was bolted into the concrete walls, a toilet, one roll of toilet tissue and a camera in the top corner of my quarters. At some point they brought in another inmate some cells further down from me.

BOOM! They closed her cell.

"Ohhhhhhh! Huh! Huh! Ohhhhhh!" She howled. "MY CATS! WHOSE GONNA FEED MY BABIES!" The individual cried out loudly.

"SHUT THE FUCK UP ALREADY!" Another inmate in a different cell shouted.

"FUCK YO-U-U-U-U!" The crying inmate responded.

Seriously? You're crying over freakin' cats? Shut the hell up for real!

At this point, reality kicked in. I was calm before this noisy woman was brought in. I glanced at the thick metal bars that were solidly embedded into the concrete walls. I'm really in fuckin' jail!

Instantly, I started to breathe heavily. I knew that if I didn't take whole of myself that I would have cracked up, so I sat upright, thought good thoughts and prayed. I asked God to relax me so I would breathe easier.

"Are you okay Nishelle?" A female officer suddenly appeared in front of my cell.

A MOTHER'S BETRAYAL

"Can you give me a blanket or something so that I can elevate my head?"

"I can't give you anything. I'm sorry," she said and walked away. I laid back down, but two minutes later, I was up again.

"Shit!" That 5 foot wooden bench was making my 5'8", 238lbs. pregnant ass extremely uncomfortable.

"You're not doing so well in there are you?" That same officer returned. Obviously the camera caught my every move.

"Not at all," I responded. Not even the pillow I made from the roll of toilet tissue helped.

"I'll be right back?" She said.

About fifteen minutes later, she returned with a sealed clear package. She tore off the wrapping and then pushed the folded plastic material through the six inch opening. After unfolding the long and wide article, I was able to bundle up the tarpaulin - creating support for my head and back.

"This is the best that I could do and if somebody asks you where you got this from – don't tell them that it was me," she seriously stated.

"Alright – thanks," I smiled.

"No problem," she walked away.

At an unknown time, several guards entered our area to serve us breakfast.

"Um! Excuse me. I don't drink coffee nor eat boiled eggs. Do you think that they can exchange this for milk and cereal?" I asked the masculine female guard.

"This is what they serve every morning - 365 days a year. Now either you drink and eat that or you don't!" *I ain't ask you all that shi*t. This, of course, was a new guard. I guess while we slept they changed shifts. Luckily for me, one of the officers at the precinct gave me his extra tuna fish sandwich prior to my transfer.

Some few minutes later, they opened the cells simultaneously, told us to step forward and to face the concrete wall in front of our cells. As one guard handed our shoes back to us, another proceeded to chain the arrestees together.

"You... because you're pregnant, you will only be chained up with one girl," the guard said. "Court begins at 9:00 A.M. sharp and I strongly suggest that you all cooperate, so you don't have to come back here later," another guard announced.

We were then taken outside and packed into a cargo van. That bitch was C-O-L-D!!! The A/C was on full blast.

My charges were 3rd degree assault and I was released on my own recognizance. I was also told that I needed a lawyer to represent me at my next court appearance. They claimed I was ineligible for a legal aid.

"Nishelle Maron." Some two hours later, the processing officer called my name. FINALLY!!!

"Here's your belongings... sign here and exit through that back door."

Lucky for me. I had $17.27 in my pocket when I was arrested, because the taxi driver charged me $12.00 to take me home that afternoon.

A MOTHER'S BETRAYAL

BOOM! BOOM! BOOM!

I knocked on the front door. During the time of arrest, I had money on me, but not my keys.

BOOM! BOOM! BOOM! I knocked again.

CLICK!

Someone unlocked the door.

"Thanks," I said as I entered the house.

"You're welcome," the Jive ass turkey responded.

The first thing I wanted to do was to jump my big ass in the shower, but I put that plan on hold in order to get a few things off my chest.

"I hope y'all had fun yesterday," I turned to him and said.

"What?" Jivasti acted as if he didn't hear me.

"I said, I hope that y'all had fun! And since people in this house are so fucked up, I just wanna let you know your marriage is based on a bunch 'a fuckin' lies! First of all, she only wants money. Remember when we needed a new stove? You know the one that only she and I contributed to because you claimed that you didn't have any money? Well, after you didn't kick in anything she told me that she was gonna make up some story to make you give her more money each month. Oh, and one more thing. Lee's not your son either," I vented.

"I know. I always had dee feeling Lee wasn't mines. And as for dee money ting, she can try if she want, 'cause I have me own stheparate sthavings account and I can leave whenever I feel like..." he said calmly while leaning up against the wall.

"...And I know 'dat she believes in 'dat shit too, 'cause I found a bottle of it in dee bedroom. It was sthome... sthome... sthome'tin dark inside of it!" He stammered.

Was this fool searching up her room? Little did he know, I heard him one day telling someone over the phone, 'you don't have to be in love wit dee person just to be wit dem.'

"Like I said in the beginning, a circus wedding. You two clowns are made for one another?" I sternly stated.

"Dem kinda tings - I don't believe in it... I mahn believe in dee almightee Jah, so she cyan't do anyting to harm me even if she tried," he preached.

A MOTHER'S BETRAYAL

"Whatever!" I left him standing there.

I went to work the next day and allowed the kids to stay in my room for the remaining of their Easter/spring break for three reasons. One – mommy's room is fun, two – a bigger bed to jump on and three – a bigger TV to watch Nickelodeon and Cartoon Network on. This I knew wouldn't totally erase that undesirable event from their innocent minds, but it would definitely alleviate the pain a little.

"Sara who put this here?" I asked her one evening after getting home from work.

"What Mommy?" She spoke from her room.

"Come here!"

"Who put this here?" I asked her again as she entered my room.

"I don't know," she responded and skipped out of my room.

Strangely, Efani's bottle of Asthma medicine was sitting on top of my dresser. *But why is this bottle even in my room*? For several moments, I stood wondering. Something told me to pick it up.

"SARA!" I shouted."YOU AND EFANI COME HERE!" As they entered my room I shook the bottle.

"AND WHERE'S THE MEDICINE THAT WAS IN IT?" I shouted again.

When I left for work that morning the bottle wasn't in my room and to my recollection it had at least 23 pills left in it. And now, the only thing inside of the bottle was the stay fresh tablet.

"I don't know!" She bucked her eyes.

"What do you mean that you don't know? Efani where's your medicine?" I interrogated them both.

"I don't know!" My four year old answered in a timid voice.

"Where are the damn tablets?" I started to panic. Every single one of the tablets were missing.

"SEARCH MY ROOM FOR THAT DAMN MEDICINE AND Y'ALL BETTER FIND IT TOO!" I yelled and threw my mattress to one side.

"Mommy, I don't see any medicine!" Sara voiced from beneath the box spring.

"Go and get the belt, because one of y'all touched that bottle and are lying." Slowly she walked out and returned with one of her belts.

"Now, I'm gonna give y'all one more chance to tell me where the medicine is....Who - touched - the medicine?"

They both shrugged their shoulders. Out of fear, anger and confusion, I hit Sara with the belt.

"NOT ME!" Sara yelled.

"So where's the medicine then?" I hit her again.

"I don't know! I don't know!" She cried out.

Feeling that she had sustained enough licks, I then turned on Efani like a mad dog. The devil was indeed working overtime. Hoping like hell that they'd tell me – never happened. Where's this medicine?

"GET YOUR COATS AND PUT THEM ON!" I shouted.

A MOTHER'S BETRAYAL

"Okay, so tell me what happened again?" The triage nurse questioned me as she checked Sara's and Efani's vital signs.

"Tonight, after getting home from work I realized that there weren't any tablets in the bottle." I repeated.

"Then what did you do?"

"I punished them because they kept telling me that they didn't know where the tablets were."

"How did you punish them?"

"With a belt."

"Who was home with them while you were at work?"

"My mother."

"Okay. Just take a seat in the waiting room and the doctor will call you," she instructed.

After being told by the doctor that my kids were fine and that they showed no signs of an overdose of any type of medication, he sent us home.

A MOTHER'S BETRAYAL

YOU - HAVE - ONE- MESSAGE. The answering machine sounded as I entered my bedroom. I hit the playback button.

"Ah! Hello Ms. Maron. This is the doctor over at the emergency room, I just examined your two children. Please. I know that it's late, but you have to bring them back because the nurse has informed me that you punished them with a belt. I'm sorry, but you have to bring them back. Thank you.

BEEP! END - OF - MESSAGES."

"Bring them back? For what?" I grew nervous and started to pace my room.

"Hello!" Renee answered in a sleepy and aggravated tone.

"Renee. It's me!"

"Girl… its 1:30 in the morning!" She grumbled.

"I know - but listen to this!" I explained the story to her from the beginning.

"You beat them? Something's telling me that your mother did away with his medicine!" Renee' speculated.

"You think so?" I asked.

"Think? Please, with the way that she thinks. I know so." There was no doubt in my cousin's mind that my mother had set me up.

"What should I do?" I asked nervously.

Take them back!" She strongly suggested.

"Take them back? But what if they take my kids away from me? I can't...."

"Did you hear what I said? Take them back because if you don't it will seem like you're running and that'll only make it worst."

"Huuuuh!" I sighed.

"Nish, hold on. I'ma call Stacey to see what she thinks about this."

CLICK. She went to her next line.

Stacey was another Maron and our 2nd cousin. We were all Pisces and the same age. For some reason, it seemed as if the younger generation Maron girls were cursed because Stacey also had experienced undesirable situations during her juvenile years. Unfortunately, this caused her to run away from home, and almost immediately, she became someone's prey. My mother allowed her little cousin to store her goods in the old van in exchange for a small fee.

For a short period of time, Stacey sold marijuana for my mother on the street corners of Brooklyn back in the mid 80's. Stacey was doing fine now and was also a mother, but that selfish situation just never left my mind because remember, I also sold drugs (cocaine) for my mother too. The only difference was that I sold it from Grams's house and I was much younger.

Upon re-entering that emergency room, my heart began to beat rapidly. Lord help me!

"Ms. Maron, thank you for coming back. I'm sorry, but if a member of our staff reports abuse we have to follow up on it," the doctor informed me.

"Abuse?" I frowned. My heart nearly stopped.

"Yes. It's just a procedure that we have to go through and it's gonna be a while, so you and your kids have a seat please."

Abuse? I can't believe this shit.

About an hour or so later, we received a visitor.

"Ms. Maron?" A woman slid back the curtain.

"Yes," I responded.

"Hi. I'm with the Department of Child Protective Services. I would like to ask you a few questions and to take a look at your kids." The short slim white woman said as she closed the curtain.

"Okay," I responded. I was a nervous wreck. Two days ago it was jail and now this.

"Are you going to take my kids away from me?" I somberly asked her.

"I know you're nervous and everything, but let me just take a look at the kids first and then we'll talk."

She pulled Efani's shirt up over his head.

"You said that you used a belt right?" The worker asked me.

"Yes," I answered her.

Right away, she pulled out her Polaroid camera and snapped a picture of his chest and back.

"Now your daughter's turn."

She pulled up Sara's shirt and also took pictures of her chest and back.

"Okay, so you realized that the medicine bottle was empty, when?"

The worker then turned and asked me.

"Yes. After I had gotten home from work."

"Who were the children with while you were at work?"

"My mother."

"Did you ask your mother if she knew where the tablets had gone?"

"No, but I grew angry and nervous and the reason for me bringing them to the hospital is because I wanted to make sure that they were okay just in case they did take the medicine." I explained to her.

"Right. And did you ever find any of the pills?"

"No. Not one." I answered and at that very moment, I noticed the police officer as he approached my curtain and stood at its opening. Jesus. They're going to take my kids away from me and I'm gonna get arrested again.

"I do see some marks on both of them from the belt, but from my experience I see no signs of abuse," she mentioned. Damn. Why did my kids have to be so pale?

"Am I getting arrested?" I then asked her.

"The officer is just part of the procedure."

Still that didn't answer my question. Talk about being a nervous wreck.

"Excuse me for just a second," the worker drew the curtain opened and walked over to the officer. I couldn't hear what they were saying, but I was praying hard that it had nothing to do with arresting me again or taking my kids away.

"Ms. Maron, I just told the officer there were no signs of abuse, so he's gonna call it in as a neglect situation. But because there are marks on the children, C.P.S. will most likely take this case to court and no...You're not getting arrested!" She smiled.

That, I realized immediately after their brief discussion because the officer walked away. Believe me, if she would have told him something otherwise, he would have taken me in with the quickness.

On April 30th, 2001 at 9:00a.m., I appeared in court with my six million dollar Italian attorney. At his request, I had to pay him $3200.00 up front for the criminal case, and after mentioning to him that I was the co-borrower on the house and wanted to remove my name from it, he agreed to start the process in Supreme Court with this same deposit. Thank God for my savings account, which was now empty because of the lawyer's fee.

"Maron vs. Maron. Step forward please!"

The court officer announced. Along with my lawyer, I approached the bench and to the right of us was - queen cobra in a red dress.

"Ladies - please raise your right hand."

The judge asked us to state our full name and address. After my lawyer and her legal aid exchanged arguments before the judge, it was stipulated that I were to remove my belongings from the house by the end of next month and an order of protection was issued against me for one year.

A MOTHER'S BETRAYAL

"Also your honor, Nishelle is a professional boxer and my client fears for her life, so we're requesting that Nishelle leave the house now!" Her legal aid attorney presented part two of his argument.

Professional boxer? He can't be possibly talking about me. I missed out on the opportunity to participate in the Golden Gloves tournament when I found out that I was pregnant with Efani months before the event, and since then, I haven't been back boxing. WOW! She is truly the devil.She obviously wasn't too satisfied with the judge's initial decision and decided to release more of her venom.

"Your honor. Where is my client supposed to go? She has no money, two children and better yet, she has another one on the way," my lawyer worked hard for his money.

"Your honor take a look at these pictures please," her legal aid handed two pictures to the court officer and she in turn handed them to the judge.

"Has the defendant seen these pictures?" The judge questioned.

"No we haven't," my attorney responded.

A MOTHER'S BETRAYAL

The judge signaled for the court officer to share the photos with us. DAMN!!! Laila Ali – you're next. She had a knot beneath her left eye and a huge bump on her forehead. Stung her ass just like I promised, but then again her lying ass probably hit herself in the head with a hammer. Crazy bitch!

"Hey! What can I say - my client's a better fighter, but in any event, her mother provoked the fight and this is unfortunately the end result," my attorney stated after viewing the photos.

"Like I said. Nishelle has a month from today to move out and an order of protection will be issued."

"But isn't it true that if Nishelle gets arrested again, her kids will be taken away from her?" My mother was now representing herself.

"You're absolutely right. If she gets re-arrested, yes her children will be taken away from her. Next case!" The judge struck his gavel.

As both parties exited the courtroom, my lawyer and I overheard a very disturbing comment.

A MOTHER'S BETRAYAL

"Well. I'll just have to get her arrested again," my mother, the very hateful and negative one said to her legal aid representative.

"Did you hear that?" My attorney fixed his eyes on me.

Instantaneously, he delicately pulled my arm indicating me to stop walking. This allowed us to create a gap between the other party and to speak without them hearing us.

"Yep!" I took a deep breath.

"Get out now! Don't wait until the month is up, because it's obvious that your mother's trying to bury you alive!" My attorney saw my mother for what she truly was."

Later that afternoon, I received a phone call.

"Hello, Nishelle Maron please!" I was about to say she's not in, because the person sounded like a bill collector - but something told me not to.

"This is she," I responded.

"This is Christian with C.P.S."

"Okay," I said.

"I was assigned to your case and I would like to stop by today for a few minutes to see the kids."

"Today?" I asked her.

"Yes, my supervisor thinks that this case will be heard in court, but until then we still have to conduct temporary home visits just to make sure that the children are fine."

"Umm… What time did you wanna come?" I asked her.

"Well, I'd like to come now if it's okay with you. It'll only take five minutes." Christian assured me. Five minutes, that's not bad. I just hope that my mother will stay in her room throughout the visit.

"Okay that's fine. I'll be looking out for you!"

"Great I'll be there in ten minutes," Christian responded. PLEEEEEZ bitch - stay up in your room!

While the kids road their bicycles up and down the street, I sat on the steps waiting nervously for Ms. Christian.

A MOTHER'S BETRAYAL

"WATCH OUT FOR THAT CAR!" I shouted as a gray Camry slowly turned onto our block.

"Why you sittin' out here?" Lee approached the house from the opposite direction.

"Nothin'. Just felt like coming outside - that's all," He took a seat on the step below me.

Go inside you little punk or go SOMEWHERE! Moments later, that same grey Camry pulled up and stopped directly in front of the house.

"Nishi - who's that white lady?" Lee asked.

"I don't know," I played it off and was hoping that he'd just go away.

"Hi Nishelle. How are you?" She greeted me as she closed her car door while holding a large manila folder in her arms.

"I'm okay," I stood up.

"Hey kids!" She smiled as she placed her right foot on the bottom step.

"Do you wanna go inside and get out of this hot sun for a while?" Christian pleasantly asked them.

"Sara - Efani. Park the bikes up for a second and come inside!" I told them.   As we entered the house I looked towards the kitchen area to make sure that the coast was clear and it was. GOOD.

"Come!" I started for my room.

"WHO ARE YOU AND WHY ARE YOU WALKING THROUGH MY FRONT DOOR?"

Out of nowhere, the serpent appeared and was now hanging her head over the staircase's railing.

"I'm here to see Nishelle and if Nishelle wishes to tell you then that's on her!" Christian snapped back.

"This is my house and I demand that you tell me who you are!" She rattled on.

"Come on!" I said and the four of us continued on to my room.

"Wh-e-w-w! So I guess that's your mother?" Christian seemed somewhat exasperated.

"Yep!" I responded and locked the door.

A MOTHER'S BETRAYAL

"I feel sorry for you!" She said. The only thing I could do was shake my head in disbelief. My mother was a ravenous beast and always on the prowl.

"Wow! What a beautiful bedroom set you have here." Christians flattering remark took my mind off of my mother's inappropriate behavior.

"Thank you!" I turned the music up a tad bit to flush out our conversation.

Christian examined the kids and spoke to me a little to get my side of the story. And just like she said, the visit was only five minutes long. The hardest part was getting her in, and then back out of the snake's pit.

"Mommy I'm thirsty!" Efani said to me.

"Okay. One minute." I told him while Christian pushed opened the screen door to leave.

"Bye kids. And Nishelle take good care of yourself okay, because you have a lot on your hands and your kids need you," she said while descending the steps.

"Thanks, and I will," I replied as she continued to make her way down..

"Mommy - I want some juice. Can I have some juice pleeeeez?" Efani started to beg.

"Me too!"' Sara joined in.

"Alright - Come on!" The three of us entered the kitchen.

"I want my rent money by the end of this week and if not - there's gonna be trouble!" My mother threatened and then went back upstairs. For a moment I just stood there thinking.

"Mommy I want some juice!" Efani was starting to get on my nerves.

I snatched the refrigerator door opened and quickly poured them both some juice. While replacing the carton, I saw today's date circled and highlighted on a calendar just to the left of the refrigerator. When I looked closer, it read SOCIAL WORKER CAME.

Sure enough Child Protective Services took the case to court. The order specified that a social worker would conduct two home visits each week for six weeks and that I would be responsible for attending and completing twelve parenting classes within that time frame. I was tired, broke, but still I had so much - my babies.

On May 24th 2001, I moved back to Brooklyn. I kept my job in Long Island hoping that the requested transfer would kick in soon.

In addition to my tiresome routine, I drove an extra ten miles east to take Sara to school. I didn't want to snatch her out when she only had five weeks left to go; it didn't make sense. Efani on the other hand, attended the daycare that was only five minutes away from my job, but after a while, my body began to show signs of a potential break down.

"Nishelle, did you put some yeast in your ankles this morning?" A co-worker was looking to get cussed out. Lucky for her, I considered her to be my friend.

"Kateera, do you still have those high water pants that you claim to be Capri's? And wait, are you wearing them now? And why do they look as if you pulled them out of a dirty laundry bag – all wrinkled up and shit," I retaliated in a joking manner.

My mind was saying that I could stick it out until my due date, but my ankles didn't. Three weeks after the move, I developed Edema. My obstetrician who was of course located in Long Island quickly put me on disability.

RING! RING! Damn! There goes my nap.

The kids and I had just returned to my basement apartment after doing some shopping at Costco one hot Sunday afternoon in July.

"Me sistren - dee baby nuh come yet?" It was the Jamaican version Renee'.

"Nah, but I had a contraction earlier."

"For real? Unoo ah guh ahv dee picknee soon den," she then happily stated.

"I hope so, 'cause I'm tired of this shit."

"You see what one night of pleasure can do for you!" Renee continued on.

"Never again girl!" I sighed.

"Dot me ah say too, cuz me nah ah'vin no more picknee fee no mahn. Two is enough for me,"

she stated.

"Yeah. I'd say the same thing if I had a kid like JuJu." I voiced.

"Whatchu mean? My son ain't bad." Renee' defended her baby.

"Did I say that?"

"No, but I know what you're tryin' to say... and he only gets smart with you because you're always fuckin' with him. That's my little pookits and he love his momma shoots." She spoke in her animated voice.

"Well, your little pookits, as you call him, is a little brat." I said.

"Yeah – okay. Well, we'll see how this Grenadian baby of yours will act when it's born, 'cause I know it's gonna come out fightin' with all the shit that you've been through."

"Whatever! You ackee and salt fish eatin', dumplin' lookin' fool. Just make sure you don't eat my child when it comes out - that's if, you're in the delivery room."

"OH, I'M GONNA BE THERE. Even if I have to take that day off from work!" Renee' was just as anxious as I was to have this baby.

"Alright, I called to check on you, and I'm gonna go now, because me and my kids have to eat. WHAT'TA

A MOTHER'S BETRAYAL

Y'ALL EATIN' TONIGHT? TOOMEY'S, CHINESE FOOD OR GLORIA'S?" Renee yelled to her pookits and his big sister.

A MOTHER'S BETRAYAL

"TRUE FRIEND"

ONLY YOU KNOW MY IN AND OUTS

*YOU KNOW WHAT I'VE BEEN THROUGH AND
WHAT I'M ALL ABOUT*

*MANY TIMES I'VE TURNED TO YOU WHEN IN A
JAM*

YOU WERE ALWAYS THERE AND GIVING A DAMN

*VERY OPINIONATED AND ALWAYS SPEAKING
FROM THE HEART*

*WHETHER GOOD OR BAD YOU ALWAYS TELL ME
WHAT YOU THINK*

*FOR SEVERAL YEARS YOU'VE DONE NOTHING
BUT CARE*

*WHICH IS WHY RIGHT NOW YOU ARE AND SHALL
FOREVER REMAIN*

MY - TRUE - FRIEND

"Whut's up? Why you holdin' you belly so?" Teddy entered the kitchen of my apartment one evening with the extra set of keys I'd given to him.

"Because earlier when I went to the bathroom I saw some blood in my panties."

"So did you call you doctor?"

"Yeah and his nurse said to go straight to the labor and delivery room."

"So why didn't you call me?" He then asked.

"I did, but your phone just rang out and I kept gettin' your voicemail."

"Alwight, I'm haye now so let's go. Sara and Efani get you shoes and put dem on." Teddy told his kids.

On our way to the hospital Teddy teased me like a big ass kid.

"Nishi, are you scared?"

"Scared of what? Shut up!" My palms were dripping wet. Hell yeah I was scared, because every pregnancy and delivery is different.

"You hands swet'tin' yet?" He continued to torment me.

"Screw you!" I laughed.

A MOTHER'S BETRAYAL

VROOM! VROOM! UR-R-R-R-R!

A biker down shifted after running a red light on Franklin Avenue.

"Look at this damn fool! Flyin' through red lights with a German on," I stated in an unpleasant tone. I sat up to get a better look at the bike.

"Teddy pull up closer so I can see what kind of bike it is."

After making the left turn onto that same street, he slowly pulled alongside that wild rider.

"It looks like a girl right?" I said to him as I leaned forward. I couldn't quite tell because it was night time.

"It's a chick. WAIT! That's Shalon. SH-A-L-O-N-N-N!" I leaned over and shouted her name through the driver's side window.

"Teddy move up some more. Hurry before the light turns green! SH-A-L-O-N-N-N!" I screamed again.

This time Teddy blew his horn. Finally, the seemingly hearing impaired rider turned around.

"Whus up Teddy! Where's Nishi?" Shalon placed her goggles on top of her helmet.

"I'm right here, you deaf ass, and what's up with you riding like that shit?"

"YO - YOU SAW THAT?" She shouted & laughed.

"We taught (thought) it was a mahn ridin' dee bike like so," Teddy said to her.

"Ha! Ha! Ha!" She laughed. "Yo - I'm so tired. I just did a double at work and I was tryin' to catch the lights, but this one caught me. Where y'all going?"

"To dee hospital," Teddy answered.

"Nish – you in labor?" She asked.

"Nah. I'm just spottin'."

BEEP! BEEP! BEEP! BBEP!

The impatient Brooklyn drivers honked.

"Call me tomorrow and let me know what's goin' on," she said and vanished into the night. She was definitely representing while I walked around resembling Bruce Bruce. Unfortunately, the spotting was just a false alarm and they sent my big ass back home.

A MOTHER'S BETRAYAL

On the afternoon of July 9th, an enormous amount of warm water gushed down my leg as I made my way to the kitchen.

"Lee. You Sara and Efani get ready, `cause I think my water just broke," I said while dialing on the phone.

"Hello," Renee' answered. She stayed home from work due to a bad case of food poisoning which caused her to have frequent anal leakage.

"My water just broke!" I spoke calmly.

"For real? Where's Teddy?" She asked.

"I don't know. But I want you to call him for me while I get my stuff and the kids ready."

"What's his cell number? Damn! Tameera ain't got home from summer school yet and her ass should'a been home by now," Renee' anxiously voiced.

"Let me go, I gotta take a quick shower too."

"SHOWER?" Renee' shouted.

"Yeah! Just because I'm pregnant doesn't mean that I have to stink."

A MOTHER'S BETRAYAL

"Whatever you do, just be careful; you don't want that baby to drop out and hit the floor. In the mean time, I'll call Teddy on his cell. Later!" Renee hung up.

"Oh, this is all baby." One of the nurses in the labor and delivery department of Methodist Hospital announced after measuring and slightly pushing down on my belly.

"I'm hot," I said to Renee' as she stood to the side of my bed.

"Yeah, it IS kinda hot in here, but the A/C is on AND the fan is blowing Nish."

"But I'm really hot Ree," I stressed to my cousin.

"Nurse," Renee' called.

"Yes?"

"She's saying that's she's extremely hot."

"The A/C's on high, but let me see if this will work," the nurse positioned the large fan directly between my colossal thighs just as another contraction came.

"She's having another contraction. OOOH! I can see the baby's head," Renee frantically voiced.

A MOTHER'S BETRAYAL

All of a sudden, that seemingly very relaxed room was transformed into a delivery room. The ceiling opened up widely and out came these huge bright lights and those fancy looking drawers were now medical trays. I had never seen anything like this before. My insurance carrier is going to get hit with a hefty bill.

"Nishelle, wait! Don't push until I tell you to. Just take deep breaths. The doctor's over in the next room and she's coming now, just breathe for me okay?" The nurse was moving fast.

"I can feel it coming out," I moaned.

"Don't push Nish, just breathe like she said," Renee' said while holding my hand.

"I am, but it's COMING! IT'S COMING!" I tried my best not to push.

"Teddy come hold her hand while I check her, 'cause these people are taking forever man," Renee' grew worried. While Renee' checked below, Teddy rubbed my head.

"NURSE!" Renee' screamed. When my cousin screamed, everyone came running in.

"Okay Nishelle, when you get another contraction – push," the doctor instructed me.

"Another one's coming now," I managed to say before the pain hit hard again.

"Okay, push and push hard!" The doctor stated.

"Mmmmm!" I closed my eyes and pushed with all my might. But when I opened them, Renee was once again by my side, and looking a bit weird.

"Nish, I gotta sit down," She spoke in a squeamish manner.

"NO! Don't leave me Ree!"

"But you don't understand, I feel like I have to faint," she swayed...

Around two something the next morning, I gave birth to an 8 lbs. 5 oz. baby boy. The biggest baby of all three and unlike the first two deliveries I received no stitches.

"Here's your baby Nishelle, give him one big welcoming kiss!" The nurse handed him over to me.

"I'll kiss him tomorrow!" I said and turned away.

The entire staff including Renee' and Teddy found

my response to be hilarious, but to me, not a damn thing was funny. Two weeks of labor pain ain't no joke. I was tired! I just wanted to sleep.

"Motorcycle here I come!" I stated as soon as I woke up later that afternoon. The room had been transformed back into its original appearance.

"You just had a baby and you're talking about a damn motorcycle? You're sick!" Renee' said. She obviously had gone home to rest, bathe, and change her clothes and to bring back Bebe's kids so that they could meet their baby cousin.

"Aww, thank you shorty!" I said to JuJu as he placed the vase filled with Chrysanthemums on my table.

"You're welcome!" My little cousin responded.

"Nishi, you had a big baby! He's so cute! His face is real big and his bottom lip sticks out just like yours," Tameera said while entering my room for the first time. Although they had been there for a while, Tameera chose to hang out at the nursery.

"Whatever!" I smiled.

"Let me go and look at my baby again!" Renee' said and headed back for the nursery.

KNOCK! KNOCK! KNOCK!

"Come in – whoever it is!" I voiced.

"What's goin' on?" It was my friend Toya.

"Hey!" I smiled.

"I hope these clothes fit him, `cause dag… that baby's big Nishi! What were you eating?" She laughed.

"Everything. So who does he look like to you?" I asked her.

"Well, I really can't tell 'cause I've only seen a picture of Teddy. And what's up with his bottom lip?" She laughed again.

"For real?" Renee' stated as she re-entered my room.

"Look! Y'all stop talkin' about my baby's big lip." I laughed with them.

"Should I tell her?" Renee, all of a sudden stopped smiling and asked Toya.

"Yeah, because I think she has the right to know," Toya responded gravely.

"Know what?" I grimaced. From the looks on their faces something was wrong.

"Your mother's here!" Renee revealed as she took a seat next to Toya.

"Don't play yourselves," I laughed.

"No. She's serious! Your mother's in the nursery feeding your baby..."